'You're trembling,' he said suddenly.

I'm not trembling because I was frightened, Lucy wanted to tell him. I'm trembling because I'm sitting here with you. I'm trembling at your touch. I'm trembling because you kissed me, because you kissed me *like that*. Rupert had kissed her like someone who had perhaps once loved her—but no longer.

Dear Reader

Welcome to Medical Romances! This month sees the innovation of an editor letter, which we hope you will find interesting and informative.

We welcome back Betty Beaty after a long absence from the list, and launch Margaret Holt with her first book, as well as offering Kathleen Farrell and Hazel Fisher—happy reading!

The Editor

Betty Beaty was born in Yorkshire and read Sociology at Leeds University. She served as a WAAF officer, became an air hostess, then worked as a medical social worker at two London hospitals and in Kent. She is married with three daughters, the youngest being a State Registered Nurse. Betty has written a number of novels, several with medical or aviation backgrounds.

THAT SPECIAL JOY

BY

BETTY BEATY

MILLS & BOON LIMITED
ETON HOUSE   18–24 PARADISE ROAD
RICHMOND   SURREY   TW9 1SR

For D—as always

First published in Great Britain 1992
by Mills & Boon Limited

© Betty Beaty 1992

Australian copyright 1992
Philippine copyright 1992
This edition 1992

ISBN 0 263 77661 1

Set in 10½ on 12½ pt Linotron Times
03-9205-43424

Typeset in Great Britain by Centracet, Cambridge
Made and printed in Great Britain

CHAPTER ONE

DOCTOR RUPERT ROXBURGH came back into Lucy Thorpe's life as suddenly and devastatingly as he had left it.

Of course the whole of the Hartington Hospital was aware that the new consultant to take charge of the obstetrics and fertility wing was due any day—a high-flyer head-hunted by the chairman of governors. But who he was and when he would come no one but the chairman knew.

Now, glancing across the clinical investigation room as the door quietly opened, Sister Thorpe saw that he had indeed come, saw the tall lean white-coated figure, the darkly handsome, once well-loved face—and her world and her heart turned upside down.

Before this sudden advent of Dr Roxburgh, Lucy had regarded her job as senior sister in charge of obstetrics and fertility as a safe and satisfying niche. The special unit was housed in the southernmost of the two wings of the Hartington, a small red-brick general hospital built on a slight rise overlooking the ever-encroaching town. The governors were forward-looking and the hospital loyally supported by the local community.

Why, Lucy cried silently to herself, as he closed

the door carefully behind him and leaned against it, why had he come back into her life? And why now?

For a second she was aware of his keen, intent scrutiny. Cold grey eyes met hers, before she lowered her gaze.

'Don't let me disturb you, Dr Duffey.' Urbanely the newcomer addressed the gowned figure seated on a stool beside the patient, nodded distantly to Lucy. 'Sister.' As if, Lucy thought bitterly, it were ever possible for Dr Roxburgh not to disturb.

Dr Duffey spun round with first a surprised, then a studiedly neutral expression on his round, usually good-humoured face. Dr Duffey, it was rumoured, had himself been a candidate for the new consultancy, made possible by a generous legacy to help further the work of in-vitro fertilisation, known to the public as 'test-tube babies'. But, rumour had it, he was not considered sufficiently forward-thrusting, and he lived apart from his wife, and that had spoiled his chances.

What sort of wife had Dr Roxburgh? Lucy wondered, avoiding his eyes. Had he married the young research doctor he had left Cambridge with four years ago? Or had he tired of her as apparently he had tired of Lucy?

Determinedly she cut short that line of thinking. She schooled her face so that neither emotion nor recognition showed. She controlled her hands so that the transfer catheter which she had just picked up stayed steady.

But what she could never control was that powerful awareness, that strange electricity that had always seemed to spark between them.

Trust him to come now, she thought, taking refuge in anger, at personally and professionally the worst time for her. Just when she had learned to forgive if not to forget him, when she had established herself in her career, when she had met a male colleague she felt she could trust, and just when she was assisting Dr Duffey in such a moving and tender operation. It was a time when even twenty-four-year-old sisters were allowed, even encouraged, to feel emotional and misty-eyed—hopefully the conceiving of a new life. If any of this showed in her large, black-lashed blue eyes, Dr Roxburgh did not appear to notice.

Advancing a few paces across the investigation-room, he put his hand briefly in a comradely fashion on Dr Duffey's shoulder. 'We have met before, Mark,' he said quietly in his deep rich voice that had now acquired a faint American drawl and intonation. 'Briefly. You came to a convention we ran at the Royal East Anglia.'

'Years ago. You have a good memory!' Dr Duffey exclaimed, looking mollified. People always did when they got the Roxburgh treatment. Even people who had been passed over for the job they wanted. 'You're the new. . .'

'Broom,' Dr Roxburgh finished, pleasantly for him.

'Oh, I didn't quite mean that.'

'I mean that,' Dr Roxburgh assured him crisply. 'I

shall be a new broom.' He smiled grittily. 'Complete with large stick and bristles.' He turned to Lucy so briefly that at the same time he turned away. 'Sister and I are old. . .' he paused '. . .acquaintances.'

Acquaintances. So that was how he described those momentous weeks, the feverish kisses, the murmurs of love. That was how he thought of her—an old acquaintance, best forgotten.

'You've been in the States, I understand,' Dr Duffey put in conversationally, perhaps sensing the tension in the atmosphere.

'At Richmond, Virginia—the Henrico Hospital. They're very advanced in their techniques there. Though we began it, of course. So I jumped at the chance of spending a few years with them.' Dr Roxburgh turned his gaze away from his colleagues to give his most beguiling smile to the patient, lying ready in the lithotomy position, her eyes bright with unshed tears, her face the colour of the sheet she had hauled up under her chin. 'And how is Mrs Bowles?' he queried.

He bent his knees and squatted on his heels so that his face was on a level with hers, conveying a seemingly effortless warmth and friendliness.

He had always been good with patients, Lucy had to concede that. The man she had learned to hate was the same one the patients seemed to learn to love. And now along with his American drawl he had brought back that specially relaxed, informal manner which so many doctors over here found it difficult to acquire. The way he looked at the patient, Mrs Bowles, the way he smiled at her, his physical nearness, did something for her, made her feel the most important person in the world.

'How am I?' Mrs Bowles repeated, a rueful smile creasing up her small, pert face. 'Frightened—very frightened, Doctor. Very.'

'Good heavens!' Rupert Roxburgh affected to look astonished. He wrinkled up his dark level brows in a typical half-humorous way that could still tear at Lucy's heart. 'That's the very last thing you should be. Excited, yes. Determined.' He put his large, well-shaped hand gently over Mrs Bowles's fist as she clutched the sheet. Lucy stared with fascination, pierced by sudden memories, as slowly and deliberately his long shapely fingers relaxed Mrs Bowles's tightly clenched ones while he talked. 'But frightened, Mrs Bowles? No. No way! That I just can't allow!'

Mrs Bowles swallowed hard. Then she confessed, 'There's something else I feel. I feel embarrassed.'

'That's just as foolish,' Dr Roxburgh told her with mock severity. 'There's nothing whatever to be embarrassed about. We're doctors; we're here to help you. We're all rooting for you. We all want you to have a baby.' His smile acquired an added friend-liness. 'What's your first name, Mrs Bowles?'

'Edna.' There was a pause. 'But I don't like it much. Then she added, 'My second name is better. My second name is Iris.'

That name again! Lucy felt a little shiver go down her spine. The name of the woman doctor Rupert had taken with him to America. It still had the power to make her feel the echo of what she had hoped was a forgotten pain.

She watched his face carefully, but insouciantly he replied, 'A lovely name, one of my favourites. And it suits you.' He patted her hand. 'I have a very close friend in the States called Iris.'

The friendliness and flattery worked. Mrs Bowles visibly relaxed. Interest and curiosity flickered in the patient's now less frightened eyes, and she even managed a faint giggle. 'A girlfriend, doctor? Or am I being the cheeky one?'

'No, Mrs Bowles, you're not being cheeky.' But he didn't answer the first question. 'Let me ask *you* a question, Mrs Bowles.'

'Of course, Doctor.'

'Are you hoping for a girl or a boy?'

'Oh, Doctor!' Mrs Bowles sighed, and turned her eyes to the ceiling. 'Either, both. Triplets, quads, quintuplets—I don't care! Just so long as I have a baby!'

Dr Roxburgh touch her cheek in an oddly tender gesture. 'Well, you will have. You must relax and believe that you will. That's half the battle.' He straightened up to his full height. 'You couldn't be in better hands.'

As almost an afterthought, he asked, 'Did your husband not want to be present?'

'No, Doctor. My Ned said he just couldn't bear to. He's a big strong man—well, Sister's seen him, so she knows. But he's a babe, a real big softie when it comes to anything medical.'

'I see,' Dr Roxburgh said, as if he didn't see at all.

Then he gave a little nod to Dr Duffey and Lucy as if indicating that the operation could now proceed, since he had done the most important part. Done it far more effectively than the mild sedative Lucy had administered, effortlessly putting the patient in a more relaxed, confident, receptive mood, thereby making the insemination more likely to succeed.

The trouble was he was right, Lucy thought resentfully. He had that special gift. He was a man who managed to be both aggressively masculine, authoritarian and at times ruthless, and yet capable of sudden disarming intuitive tenderness. A powerful mixture. And perhaps that was partly what had deluded her before. Perhaps that spark of awareness and understanding that had seemed to be for her and for her alone was for all women, part in fact of his medical repertoire.

The slight scraping of the stool as Dr Duffey moved closer to the patient brought Lucy guiltily out of her momentary reverie. At a nod from him, she told Mrs Bowles, 'If you'd just turn a little further on your side. . .that's right. Thank you, Mrs Bowles. Splendid! Draw your left leg a little further up!' She handed the transfer catheter to Dr Duffey and pulled the sheet further back.

'Mrs Bowles,' Dr Duffey leaned close, 'just try to relax your muscles! Don't tense up! I'm going to insert this catheter in your uterine cavity. It won't hurt, I promise you. You may get a sensation of cold, and in a little while you may feel some cramps, but that's all, and they'll soon pass.'

Lucy moved a pace to stand at Mrs Bowles's head. Mrs Bowles stretched up the hand that Dr Roxburgh had unclenched and Lucy squeezed it. 'I'm not frightened any more,' she whispered, 'just frightened it won't succeed, like everything else before.'

Lucy's blue eyes softened. For fifteen years Mrs Bowles had undergone every known test and treatment for infertility. Lucy studied the patient, willing this treatment to succeed. She even forgot Rupert Roxburgh watching everything like a white-coated hawk. Eyes downcast, full curving mouth tremulous, fine fair hair scooped up smoothly under her surgical cap; it seemed strange that Dr Roxburgh's eyes should so harden when he allowed them to rest momentarily on her. If there was hostility, it was by no means only hers.

Mrs Bowles gave a little gasp, then took a sharp indrawn breath.

'There, that's all done!' Dr Roxburgh came forward as if *he* had performed the simple operation and stood right beside Lucy. Their arms touched, and she drew away.

'After this, we want you to rest for half an hour,' Dr Duffey put in with a slightly exasperated glance up at Dr Roxburgh. 'You must try not to move. Sister will close the blinds in a moment. Think nice pleasant romantic thoughts!'

'Erotic thoughts!' Dr Roxburgh corrected him.

'Think about your big strong Ned. Imagine you're in his arms. Feel him close. I'm not joking, I'm deadly serious. This is an important moment. Share it in your mind with your husband. Desire him. But when you get home, remember, no sexual intercourse till we've established whether or not you're pregnant.'

He patted Mrs Bowles's hand, then stepped back a pace. 'Now Sister will see you stay calm and comfortable.'

'I'm sure she will. She's sweet,' said Mrs Bowles.

Dr Roxburgh raised his brows but made no comment. He turned towards the door. Over his shoulder, as an apparent afterthought, he said, 'Sister. . . Dr Duffey. . . I'd like a quick meeting. Four o'clock. Your office will do, Sister.'

No 'may we use your office?' No 'is that convenient?' Just throwing his weight around, giving orders. The new broom sweeping abrasively clean.

'The shape of things to come!' Dr Duffey smiled wryly over his shoulder as they scrubbed up. His brows lifted in concern to his light ginger hair. 'You were acquaintances,' he said. 'How well did you know him before?'

'He was the registrar, a very up-and-coming registrar at the Royal East Anglia. That was before he got this offer from the Henrico, and I was only a second-year nurse.'

'So he didn't stoop to conquer?' Dr Duffey fancied himself as a literary buff.

Lucy laughed as if it were a joke, and pulled down the blinds with finality.

It was much less easy to pull down the blinds on Mrs Bowles. She had the brightest, most ferreting brown eyes that Lucy had ever seen, and she was experiencing that euphoria which all patients went through after the embarrassing little operation was done.

'Now he really is the dishy doctor,' she began invitingly. 'So tall, isn't he? Must be well over six feet. Taller than Ned—six foot three I'd say, Sister, wouldn't you?'

'About that.'

'Good build too—muscular, strong shoulders. I could fancy him myself if it wasn't for my Ned!'

'Tell me about Ned,' Lucy suggested. 'Where did you meet?'

'Work. I was an accounts clerk with the railway, and Ned's a driver. We met in the office.' And all in the same breath, 'Do you fancy him?'

'Him?'

'The dishy doctor.'

It was always the same, Lucy well knew. Patients wanted to talk about *your* love-life. Charles Waters, the senior counsellor, had recently given a lecture to the unit saying patients should be encouraged to talk and to ask seemingly impertinent questions, because it made them feel happier and more relaxed and more likely to conceive.

'No, I don't!' Lucy denied indignantly. 'I certainly don't. Quite the opposite. I admire his skill—he's a superb doctor. But. . .as a man!'

Mrs Bowles laughed softly and knowingly, but said nothing.

After a moment she asked, 'You're not married, are you?'

'No.'

'Engaged?'

'No.'

'Living with anyone? I mean, lots of girls do nowadays, don't they?'

Lucy shook her head. 'I share a small house with two colleagues.'

'Girls?'

''Fraid so,' Lucy sighed humorously.

'But I bet you have lots of boyfriends!'

'Enough to be going on with,' Lucy laughed.

'Anyone special?'

'Now that's a difficult question.'

If you'd asked me that a month ago, Lucy thought, the answer would have been no. Now she added, 'I'm not sure.'

Mrs Bowles sighed. 'I was sure with my Ned the moment I saw him. Eyes across the room—the desk, in this case. Drawn to each other. It really was like that. Magnetised, we were, hypnotised, like someone winding in a reel. There, you don't believe me! I can tell by your face.'

Oh, but you're wrong, Mrs Bowles, Lucy wanted to cry out. I believe you. That's what *I* felt once. His eyes across the room at the hospital dance, knowing he was going to come over, seek me out as inexorably as if there was no one else in the room, or in the whole world. Sitting beside Mrs Bowles, she could almost feel his encircling arms, the touch of his strong fingers, feel again her whole being deceiving her that this sensation was special to them both.

Aloud she said, smiling. 'I do believe you, Mrs Bowles. You do seem made for each other. You're very lucky. I've talked to Mr Bowles, don't forget.'

'Of course,' Mrs Bowles smiled reminiscently, 'you counselled us; set us on our way, as it were. You and that nice Dr Waters.'

Lucy felt her cheeks colour, and immediately Mrs Bowles noticed the tell-tale flush and pounced. 'Is that him? The one you might be interested in? Ooh, how thrilling!'

Thrilling was not the word to describe the tender shoot of Lucy's relationship with Dr Charles Waters. Soothing, restrained, sensible, supportive. But at twenty-four, Lucy had decided to put thrills and passions behind her. Those belonged to the now almost forgotten era of Rupert Roxburgh. It had taken her three years to reckon she could trust a man again, and she was just beginning to believe that Charles was such a man. Not that two dinner dates and a day exploring the Dorset coastline constituted a relationship, and not that she had wasted the intervening few years.

Not for nothing had Dr Roxburgh once called her his fire-and-ice maiden. Her wide and innocent blue eyes, her calm smooth brows were balanced by a passionate mouth which once he had called wayward, and a small, pointed but very determined chin.

When the affair with Rupert came to a brutal end, she would not allow herself to mope. She threw herself into her work, finished her nursing degree. Then she had taken a post-graduate course in in-vitro fertilisation, and another in counselling. The doctors recognised her as a lynch-pin in the unit.

Lucy checked her watch. Half an hour had gone by. She walked over to the window and pulled up the blinds. Afternoon sunlight flooded in. It gleamed on the little statue of Eros, god of love and fertility, given by a patient for the small rose-garden just outside. It lit the spring green leaves of the beeches in the hospital garden and gilded the cupola on the distant university building in the centre of the town.

'Oh, is it that time already? I'm sorry it's over.' Mrs Bowles sounded quite disappointed, but heal-thily relaxed. 'And you've not had time to tell me more about that nice Dr Waters.'

At that precise moment Dr Waters put his head round the door. 'Did I hear my name being taken in vain?'

Quite unlike Dr Roxburgh, he didn't come barg-ing in, but paused till Lucy beckoned him inside. He was a slim man of a little above average height in his early thirties. A lock of light brown hair fell over his high forehead, as if attempting to disguise its intelli-gence. His hazel eyes were watchful, his mouth firm and full, but frugal with its smiles. His appearance was attractive. He always dressed impeccably. He was an attentive escort. And yet. . .

'Yes,' Mrs Bowles told him cheekily as he closed

the door behind him, 'you did hear your name. *I* said it. And did you hear what I called you?'

Charles shot an amused glance at Lucy. 'Not exactly.'

'I called you that nice Dr Waters. And I meant it.'

He gave her a little bow. 'Thank you—I'm grateful.'

'And I'm grateful to you, Dr Waters, for your counselling. I can't see my Ned talking about that sort of thing to anyone else, really I can't.' Mrs Bowles turned to Lucy. 'Shall I dress now?'

'Yes, do. I'll just wheel you round the screen. Your husband's waiting in the reception hall.'

'Bless him,' Mrs Bowles sighed as Lucy wheeled her behind the screen. 'We'll be living on pins for the next fortnight. He's as keen on this baby as I am.'

Charles turned to Lucy. 'It's eight minutes to four,' he reminded her. 'The meeting's at four.'

'I know.'

'I thought when you're ready I'd walk you round to your office.'

'Thanks,' Lucy smiled. 'Safety in numbers?'

'No, not really. I just wondered if you knew why. Why the Big White Chief has suddenly called a meeting.'

Lucy shook her head, and called, 'Are you ready, Mrs Bowles?'

'Here I am!' Mrs Bowles came teetering from behind the screen on three-inch heels, and wearing a tight short skirt that further hampered her movements. She shook hands with both of them. 'See you soon, I hope. Keep your fingers crossed for me. Next time I see you, let's hope it's the ultra-scan, eh?'

'I'll keep my fingers crossed.' Lucy smiled. 'Good luck!'

'Something tells me we're all going to need a spot of luck.' Charles put his hand on her shoulder as they turned the corner into the small corridor that led to her room. Then he bent down and kissed the tip of her nose.

'I can see that you and I will have to stick together. First day here,' he said, 'and already the new White Chief is making waves.'

Exactly the height and strength of those waves, Charles Waters would have no idea, Lucy thought, but she simply nodded.

'I'll just pop into my office for my notes.' Charles patted her affectionately on the shoulder. 'Be with you in a tick!'

Lucy had scarcely seated herself in her office when a peremptory knock sounded on the door, and a dark head appeared round it before she had time to call, 'Come in!'

'Dr Waters not here, Sister?'

'He's just getting his notes.'

'Dr Duffey not here either?'

'As you see.'

Just for a wild moment, she thought he might have come a little early to speak to her alone. To remember, to reminisce. But the irritated frown that drew together his black brows disabused her.

There was a knock on the door, and a pause. Charles Waters was always polite.

'Come in, Charles,' Lucy called.

He came in smiling. Dr Roxburgh looked at his watch, then said, 'Don't bother to sit down, Dr Waters. There's just one thing I'd like to say to you. In future, I want you to ensure the presence of the patient's husband at inseminations. Is that clear?'

Charles frowned. 'I did my best.'

'Obviously not good enough. A woman needs her husband at such a time. I believe it's of prime importance. Please remember that.'

He's making an enemy, Lucy thought, as Dr Waters silently left the room. Charles doesn't take kindly to criticism. Rupert Roxburgh's making too many waves.

The door suddenly opened again, and Dr Duffey hurried into the room without troubling to knock. 'Sorry I'm a few minutes late.'

'A few minutes,' Dr Roxburgh corrected him. 'Seven, to be precise.'

'I had a somewhat verbose patient,' Mark apologised, running his fingers through his rumpled ginger hair. 'You know the sort, Rupert.'

'I do indeed, Dr Duffey. I also know how to terminate the consultation.'

'It's a knack,' Lucy said drily, 'that comes with age and experience,' and saw Mark shoot her a grateful glance, and Dr Roxburgh give her a sharp reproving one.

'Well, now, don't let's waste any more of our mutually valuable time.' Dr Roxburgh consulted his wrist watch. 'I want a brief post-mortem on Mrs Bowles's insemination.'

Lucy and Mark exchanged puzzled, defensive glances.

'Any particular reason?' Mark wrinkled up his forehead, a dark flush spread over his face to the roots of his hair.

'I rarely do anything without a reason.' Dr Roxburgh sat back in his chair and crossed one leg over the other. 'First of all, the patient was about as relaxed as a violin string. Oh, I know it's difficult, but not impossible. You were far too tense, Dr Duffey. As for you, Sister. . .!'

So it went on. With difficulty, Lucy restrained herself. Dr Roxburgh had always been high-handed, but now the years spent turning himself into one of the leading experts on infertility, qualifying medically and surgically, had given him an insufferable arrogance. Yet for all his knowledge of the latest techniques and thinking, he was still a man. He could never really understand.

Suddenly he turned to her again. 'What semen did you give Mrs Bowles, Sister?'

'Donor X. His physical characteristics match the Bowles's well.'

'And he's had a good success rate,' Dr Duffey put in.

'I don't think any fertililty unit has a good enough success rate.'

'We're all working on it.' Dr Duffey looked more than ever like a ruffled teddy bear.

'Just as we are now,' Dr Roxburgh responded grittily. 'We have to examine every case and see how we can better it. You'll have read the report of the British Licensing Authority. More effort needed.' He gave them both a frosty smile. 'So let's start as we mean to go on. Sister, in my opinion you should have made a mixture of Mr Bowles' sperm and donor X's.'

'But. . .' Lucy began to protest.

'For two reasons,' Dr Roxburgh settled back in his chair, and held up two fingers of his right hand, ignoring her interruption. 'One, because in my opinion it increases the chance of success.'

'But his count was one of the lowest we've ever had!' Lucy expostulated.

'I'm quite aware of that. But research has shown it can increase the chances.'

This was where Lucy Thorpe was on familiar ground. This was her subject, her expertise, her compensation perhaps, some might say. 'I've read that research paper,' she said. 'It's Cooper, Baltimore '89. I think it's inconclusive.'

'You're entitled to think whatever you like, Sister. But while I'm in charge, we'll run the unit my way.'

Dr Roxburgh put down one finger to show that point one was taken care of.

'Secondly, the psychological effect.' He turned to

her, his grey eyes cold and hard. 'Have you anything to say on that, Sister?'

'Not at the moment.'

'Well, then, if I say bonding, doesn't the psychological advantage spring to mind?'

'Perhaps,' Lucy murmured cautiously.

Dr Duffey, to whom the new director turned his eyes, said tactfully, 'Well, yes, I think I know what you're getting at.'

'I'm saying that such an insertion means the baby could be Mr Bowles's.'

'I disagree.'

Dr Roxburgh gave Lucy the benefit of a long, slow stare. She felt a little shiver run down her spine of mingled anger and excitement. It was a powerful, frightening mixture. She clenched her fists and prepared for a sharp put-down, but none came.

He drew a deep breath as if to summon up hidden reserves of much-needed patience. 'I said *could*, Sister. In my experience, the bonding process is much helped. It's a psychological factor that can't be ignored.

'Dr Duffey,' he switched his eyes from her to Mark, 'when you were at school did you play team games, hurdle, cross-country?'

'Yes, I did.'

'Sister,' he turned to Lucy, 'I know you were part of the Royal East Anglia team we sent to the marathon.'

She flushed. She felt tears spring to her eyes that he remembered, and a sudden deep, dark anger that he should toss up these memories so casually and uncaringly.

'I remember cheering you on,' he added. 'You finished.'

'I finished, yes. No way up front, though.'

'But other people spurred you on, Sister? Dr Duffey?

They both nodded.

'It's unlikely you'd have simply done these activities so competitively otherwise.' He turned to Lucy again. 'Do you get my point, Sister?'

'Yes, I do,' she answered slowly.

'Who is to say which seed raced first to the oocyte? And psychologically that's a factor which helps enormously in the parent-child bonding process.'

'But. . .' Lucy began.

'Yes, Sister. But what?'

'The parents could have——'

'A blood test and find out?' He took the words from her. 'Sure they could. But not even that would be for certain. And in practice, they don't. Some of them,' his voice subtly changed, 'believe it's the love between them that's important. They're content to leave the rest a mystery.'

For a brief second his expression softened. His eyes rested on Lucy, but he didn't seem to see her. To Mark Duffey, she made a lovely picture with the slanting afternoon sun glittering on her smooth fair hair, turning her eyes to sapphire in her pale, delicate face. But to Dr Roxburgh it served only to remind him of time. His expression returned to its normal severity.

'Time of day,' he said suddenly and crisply. And when the other two looked at him questioningly, 'I believe time of day assists conception. The evening works best.'

'But I thought that wasn't proved,' Lucy exclaimed. 'Maxwell and Morgan. . .'

Dr Roxburgh looked exasperated. '. . .were not able to prove it conclusively,' he finished for her. 'But they found sufficient pointers. Sufficient for me.' And in the same breath, 'Why do you always argue, Sister?'

'I wasn't aware that I did.'

'Then let me point out to you that *you do*. Or so my experience so far has shown me.' He gave her a faint, acid smile to show that his reproof was tinged with humour.

'Anyway,' she went on with daring, tilting her pointed little chin and eyeing him squarely, 'I consider it an experienced sister's duty so to argue. To put another point of view.'

'Do you indeed?' He raised one black eyebrow. 'But in this case are you experienced enough to argue with me?' He didn't give her time to reply. 'Whether you are or not,' he went on sharply, 'we shall do as many of these inseminations as possible in the evening.'

'It will create difficulties with the nursing schedule,' Lucy protested doggedly.

'Well, I'm sorry to upset your social life, but that's what I intend.'

And with that, Dr Roxburgh terminated the meeting, if that was what it could be called.

'I don't think he means to be quite such a martinet,' Dr Duffey remarked pacifically, as Lucy made a reviving cup of tea. 'According to the grapevine, he has personal problems. *Cherchez la femme*. He's been on the transatlantic phone to the Henrico already. *La femme* in question is a girl called Iris.'

CHAPTER TWO

THE name of Iris cropped up later that evening at Three, Laburnum Villas, a small Edwardian terraced house twenty minutes' walk from the Hartington Hospital which Lucy shared on a furnished tenancy with two other girls—Fenella Jeffreys, a physiotherapist in the cardiac wing, and Meg Mullins, a sister on Maternity who always knew everything before it happened. The name of Iris cropped up, as Lucy might have expected, bracketed with Dr Roxburgh's.

Meg was the outgoing, bubbly one of the trio. 'Sure, it's all over the hospital,' she announced as she stir-fried the vegetables for the evening meal. 'If he's not engaged to this Iris, married even, he soon will be. And why not? Doesn't it stand to reason by the law of luck and averages? A man like himself would never be free. And wouldn't we be the just too lucky ones if he was?'

She lifted the wok off the gas ring and spooned the savoury-smelling mixture on to a dish.

As the three of them settled round the table, the talk continued on the new consultant.

'He came round this afternoon,' Meg said, 'and all the young mums drooled.'

'I don't believe it,' Lucy protested briskly.

27

'Ask Mrs Bowles.' The smile on Meg's round rosy face broadened. 'She popped in to make sure we'd have a bed in nine months' time.'

'I wish they wouldn't do that!' Lucy frowned.

'So do I, and so I told her. Don't count your chicks—literally. But they won't be told.' Meg's smile faded and her grey eyes clouded. 'They just won't listen. She went round talking to the mums and peeping at the babes, till Dr Roxburgh came in and said everything I'd said, but this time with that special way of his. And hey presto, she took it in, metaphorically kissed the hem of his garment and departed.'

'The great man hasn't yet paid us a call,' Fenella said. At twenty-eight she was the oldest of the four—tall, with short-cropped hair and large mournful eyes. She had originally wanted to be a ballet dancer, but had grown too tall. She had been married to a fellow physiotherapist—a well-known amateur climber who had been killed in the Alps six months later. She never spoke of him except to say that no man could possibly live up to him, and so she could never marry again.

Lucy in her own way was just as reticent about her early years—an only child, left at a small girls' boarding-school, while her parents were in South America on engineering projects similar to the dam her father was at present building in Peru. 'Cardiac rehab is a bit out of his territory,' said Meg, scraping the last of the vegetables on to Fenella's plate, 'but if what I hear is correct, he's going round the whole hospital winning friends and influencing people.'

'He certainly seems to have won you,' Fenella said.

'At first sight.'

'But you're a pushover.' Fenella gave Meg one of her rare smiles. 'The wonder is that Andrew puts up with you.'

Andrew was literally the boy next door. For Number One, Laburnum Villas was rented by male hospital staff—Andrew, who was chief technician at the seminology lab, Mick, who was an electronics wizard, and Jim, a radiographer. Their presence was invaluable because, like many hospitals these days near town centres, the Hartington suffered from prowlers round the nurses' quarters. Andrew and Meg had been going out together for some time, and he always made his return from the laboratory known by a short sharp burst on the horn of his motorbike.

Meg allowed the conversation at the rest of supper to drift away from the subject of Dr Roxburgh and on to the new sit-com that had just started on ITV the previous night. But afterwards, when Fenella was writing letters in their sitting-room, and she and Lucy were washing up in the kitchen, she returned to it with what she clearly thought was the best piece of gossip she'd managed to glean that day.

'Mrs Bowles said you and Dr Roxburgh had met,' she remarked.

'Ages ago, when I was still a student at the Royal

East Anglia and he was. . .' Lucy spread her hands to indicate the width of the gap between them '. . .the registrar.'

'And you fell for him, of course,' Meg persisted. It was a statement more than a question.

'I was young.'

'Ah,' Meg gave a derisively exaggerated sigh, 'the universal explain-all! Did he date you? Or was it just eyes across the ward, cardiac fibrillation and the touch of an antiseptic hand?'

Lucy laughed, as she was meant to. 'Oh, no, we dated all right.'

'Passionate embraces? Or just a goodnight kiss?'

'Not just a goodnight kiss.'

'So then?'

'Then another woman.'

'It happens. And. . .?'

'Off to America.'

'With her?' queried Meg.

'Yes, with her.'

'Could it be a woman called Iris?'

'Yes, it could. Still. . .' Lucy bit her lip, drew in her breath and tried to look as if it was all water under the bridge. 'He taught me a valuable lesson. Never trust a man.'

'Sound advice.' Meg smiled as suddenly from the street below came the sound of a motorcycle engine and the enthusiastic hoot of a horn. 'Well, there's Andrew. I must love you and leave you. I'm tempted to trust *him* sometimes, but I shall remind myself to resist.'

Later that night, just after midnight, she knocked on Lucy's bedroom door and in answer to a sleepy, 'Come in, if you must,' skipped over to subside on Lucy's bed.

She reached out and switched on the bedside lamp. 'My resistance was low, and what there was, Andrew overruled,' she confessed. 'I've been persuaded to trust him.'

She thrust her left hand into the pink radiance of the lamp, so that it could sparkle on the little circlet of diamonds. 'My Andrew popped the question, complete with ring. Congratulate me, Lucy! Hugs and kisses are in order!'

'Oh, I do congratulate you!' Lucy hugged her. 'Andrew's super! We all love him like a brother. And after all, there's an exception to every rule!'

'An exception to every rule'—those were the same words that Lucy used again three evenings later, but in a very different context and in a tone much more defensive than to Meg. It was in the theatre proper of the fertility unit where Lucy was about to assist Dr Roxburgh in an IVF operation—the implantation of a cluster of fertilised oocytes in the womb of a thirty-nine-year-old Yorkshirewoman, Mrs Doreen Armitage. Already Dr Roxburgh had put into effect his dictum of evening oocyte implantation, believing that better results were thus attained. In many hospitals IVF was known not by those initials but as LR— Last Resort. 'By my rules,' Dr Roxburgh told Lucy as they scrubbed up, 'I would have excluded Mrs

Armitage. But there's an exception to every rule,' he echoed her sardonically. Then he asked, 'Mark Duffey did the first laparoscopy?'

'Yes.'

Dr Duffey, Lucy knew, always erred on the side of optimism, of giving the patient another chance. But Dr Roxburgh was a different, harder, more ruthless man.

'I would have hesitated because of tubular occlusions,' he went on. 'But Mark thought it was worth the chance?'

'Yes.'

'I presume the exception to every rule was Dr Duffey's dictum?' he persisted.

'Yes.'

'What was your opinion, Sister?'

'I think she has a chance.'

'But a remote one?'

'I'm not really qualified to say.'

'How touchingly modest and loyal! But come, Sister! You're highly qualified and experienced. Did you have doubts?'

Lucy set her mouth stubbornly and kept rebelliously silent. Nothing would induce her to be disloyal to Dr Duffey, and nothing would induce her to say anything to ingratiate herself with such a man as Dr Roxburgh.

He didn't press her, and made no further comment. 'Both you and Dr Waters were impressed with the Armitages. Dr Waters initiated the counselling?' he asked.

'Yes to both questions. In fact, Mrs Parsons also did a counselling session with Mrs Armitage.'

'Would you be surprised if I said that in my opinion, in my *medical* opinion, despite their determination to become parents the treatment may be doomed to failure?'

'No, not surprised,' Lucy said tersely. 'But hopeful that you're wrong.'

For a moment, Dr Roxburgh looked astonished that anyone could consider that possibility, then he asked, 'You were present at the oocyte collection with Dr Duffey?'

'Yes.'

'So you know there was some tubal occlusion?'

'Yes.'

'So it's doubtful I'm wrong.'

Lucy said nothing. Dr Roxburgh simply raised his brows and studied the notes. 'And the oocytes were left to mature for six hours? Good! Then sperm insemination. And the cells have now satisfactorily multiplied. The husband's sperm only was used?'

'Yes.'

'Is the lab report on his semen here? Ah, yes! I see. . . Semen wash with antibiotics in the culture medium. Good! And is Mr Armitage here?'

'He didn't want to be present at the insemination. He asked if we'd see him afterwards.'

'Very well.' Dr Roxburgh pulled on his surgical gloves. 'Let's get it done.' He walked through to the treatment-room—and it was as if along with his surgical gloves, he pulled on the well-known charm.

'Mrs Armitage.' He smiled at the patient lying ready under the sheet. 'I'm sorry we haven't met before, but I've only been here a few days and your IVF course had already begun. I shall look forward to meeting Mr Armitage.'

He pulled up his stool confidentially close. 'For you, the worst part is over, Mrs Armitage. Patients usually dislike the laparotomy the most. And of course all the prodding and examining. But this will be quite painless. The more relaxed you are the better. Just consciously let your muscles go! Turn over a little. No, there's no need to hold Sister's hand! Let your hand go limp.' He held out his own hand for the transfer catheter, bent over Mrs Armitage and neatly slipped it in. 'Well done, Mrs Armitage!'

'Is that all there is to it, Doctor?'

'That's all.'

'And am I pregnant?'

Dr Roxburgh shook his head. 'There are fertilised cells now inside you. It's up to your body to choose to host them.'

'Oh, it must!'

'We hope so, but no one can tell. So rest and relax now. But try not to move. Sister will shortly turn down the lights.'

He bent and whispered in the patient's ear.

'Yes, Doctor,' she said, looking up at him with wide eyes, 'if you say so. Oh, and Doctor—it's kind of you to see my husband.'

'Think nothing of it. Sister and I won't be able to

see him for a while. I have a patient to examine in the main hospital in between.'

'That's very good of you. Being so much older than me, he seems to worry even more.'

As they walked out of the unit together, Dr Roxburgh said, 'I'd like you with me when I have this talk with Mr Armitage. You're not in a hurry, I hope?'

'Not particularly,' Lucy told him.

'No boyfriend waiting?'

'No.'

'You surprise me.' He seemed about to ask another question, thought better of it, then added, 'I know it's getting late. I'll try to see Armitage doesn't keep us too long.'

But Mr Armitage was a very anxious and a very determined man. He was a well-preserved ruddy-faced tycoon in his sixties who had built up a huge international clothing and textile empire, as he said 'out of nowt'. For years his wife and he had wanted a family, and this, seemingly, they couldn't have. They'd consulted doctors all over the world—with the net result of much stress for his wife, but no heir for him or his firm.

He was in the reception hall, leafing through magazines, when Lucy went through to collect him. He got to his feet, a big lumbering man with a jutting jaw and thick brows over small shrewd eyes.

'Grand of you to spare the time, lass!' He grasped her hand. 'You work hard, I'll say that!' he

smoothed the few strands of hair over his bald dome
and asked, 'How's my wife?'

'She's very comfortable. She's just been resting.
Now you can take her home.'

'Champion!' He looked relieved. 'And where's
the doctor?'

'He'll be along shortly. We'll go and wait in my
office.'

Lucy took him along the corridor and had scarcely
settled him into a comfortable chair when, after a
perfunctory knock, Dr Roxburgh came in.

'Ah, there you are!' he exclaimed, as though they
had somehow been hiding themselves away. 'Can
you rustle up some coffee for us, Sister?' He went
over and shook Mr Armitage's hand. 'Now what did
you particularly want to ask us?'

There was only one question, now he knew his
wife was all right, that Mr Armitage wanted to ask,
and when Lucy returned with the coffee and handed
them the cups, he was still asking it.

'Now you've done it, can you tell me if it's going
to work?'

Lucy glanced at Dr Roxburgh's stern face.

'I can tell you in one word. No, Mr Armitage, I
can't tell you if it's going to work.'

'It must, Doctor!'

'Only time will tell.'

'Nay, lad, it must work! It's gotta be a success!'

Lucy glanced sideways at Dr Roxburgh's face. His
level brows were drawn close together, his mouth
set in a straight uncompromising line, but his eyes

held sympathetic understanding as he spoke quietly to the man seated opposite him, the cup of coffee untouched by his side.

'No, Mr Armitage, there's no such thing as must. We. . .myself, Sister,' he threw Lucy a brief abstracted look, 'the whole staff. . .lab technicians, seminologists, embryologists, the anaesthetists, the nurses. . .all want it to work. But no one can say it will. Remember, Mr Armitage, man proposes, God disposes.'

'Aye, you're right! But my wife—by heck, the poor lass has been through so much!'

'They all go through so much. That's why we only take on those with the guts and patience to go through with it, as I'm sure you have. And Mrs Armitage.'

'All those examinations! I didn't like what I had to go through. No man would, by heck! But she had far more! Then the injections. She got headaches. And a bright red rash.'

'The hCG injections, the lutein-inducing drugs?' Dr Roxburgh nodded sympathetically. 'There are side-effects sometimes, but not with everyone. Putting up with them is all part of the commitment. You see, in order for couples to have a baby this way, they have to show tremendous courage, love, respect, restraint and support for one another.'

Lucy watched Dr Roxburgh curiously. Gone was the ambitious, stern and arrogant consultant, and in his place was a keen, compassionate doctor who believed ardently in what he was doing.

'People used to say in the past that this method of fertilisation was unnatural. But who's to say that all this love and understanding that couples need to have to support one another is less natural than the physical act of love? So many babies are conceived carelessly and unlovingly, for the passion of the moment, while these IVF babies are born into love.'

'I'm with you there, Doc, one hundred per cent! It's not what goes on between the sheets but between the parents, eh?'

Dr Roxburgh looked startled for a moment, but then nodded sagely.

'And there's a lot we could give a child, if only we could have it,' Mr Armitage went on. 'And I don't mean just money! But this is one thing you can't buy, eh, Doctor?'

Despite Mr Armitage's philosophical approach, he went on telling them about the advantages he would hope to give a child. He had sweated a lifetime to build up his vast clothing and textile empire, but he had no heir, not even a nephew or niece or cousin. If IVF failed, someone had told him something about GIFT. What about that?

'Gamete Interfallopian Transfer,' Dr Roxburgh frowned. 'That means placing both gametes into the ampullary section of the fallopian tubes.' He shook his head.

'Why not, Doctor?'

'Because of abnormalities in your wife's fallopian tubes.'

Mr Armitage sighed and shook his head. 'So nothing might work?'

'I'll be frank, Mr Armitage. Your semen counts, the tests and the laparoscopy have given indications of why your wife doesn't conceive. My opinion now is that the chances of this latest attempt are not high. I myself, if the decision had been mine, might not have accepted her for the programme. But I'm glad that Dr Duffey has given her that chance.'

Mr Armitage sat silent. Then he said, 'Thanks for giving it to me straight from the shoulder, for calling a spade a spade.' He drew in a deep breath and mopped his forehead with his handkerchief. 'Could she have another attempt if this fails?'

Patiently Dr Roxburgh, the kindly compassionate doctor, explained again the stresses, both mental and physical, of the programme, ending with, 'You'll appreciate that repeated hormonal stimulation, and yet another programme, might not be wise.'

It was well after ten when Mr Armitage finally got slowly to his feet and clapped Dr Roxburgh on the shoulder.

'Thanks, Doc. You're an honest man—I like that. You've told me straight. I can face facts. What I can't stand is shilly-shallying and soothing claptrap.'

When the door closed behind him, Dr Roxburgh turned to Lucy. 'I'll see you home,' he said. 'Get your coat. My car's outside.'

Lucy tilted up her chin. 'It's all right, I prefer to walk. I'm used to walking.'

'I don't care what you're used to. It's dark, and it's late. I'm driving you home. Don't argue!'

Lucy didn't argue. She simply walked to her reception office, lifted her coat off the peg, and left the hospital by the main door. Nothing could have induced her at that moment to endure the proximity of Rupert Roxburgh. She was tired. She was keyed up. And, for all her protestations to herself that she had got over him, she found his physical presence profoundly disturbing.

Outside the night was cool. It swallowed her up. There was no moon and only a handful of stars. But the very darkness was strangely soothing and afforded an illusion of protection, and anonymity.

It was as if she could hide away—from him and from her feelings for him. The shadows cast by the lines of little dark terraced houses seemed like a burrow down which she could hurry to escape.

She walked briskly, the click of her footsteps echoing over the pavements. Cars passed, momentarily drenching her in the white light of their headlamps. She was not aware of being nervous, though these days all female staff had been advised to walk in pairs or in groups. Dear kind Andrew or Mick or Jim from next door were always ready to escort anyone coming off late shift, especially about the time the pubs came out.

Lucy had just passed the most notorious local. A bunch of sweat-shirted youngsters were downing ale in the doorway and shouting out to any female that went by, when she became aware that there was an echo to her footsteps.

Ahead lay Laburnum Road, which in turn gave way to Laburnum Villas. It was a dark road of tightly terraced houses, locked front doors and sooty rhododendrons.

She hurried. The footsteps hurried too.

She slowed. The footsteps slowed.

She listened carefully. Two pairs of footsteps. Two padding pairs of footsteps.

She dipped her right hand into her coat pocket and gripped her keys, the only weapon she had.

When it happened, it all happened very quickly. Suddenly the footsteps behind slithered into a soft run. One moment her mind registered that fact. The next, before she'd time to turn, an arm was round her neck. Another twisted her right hand behind her back.

A broken beer bottle was thrust into her face.

Then as suddenly as if they were a scene to be spotlit on a stage they were all bathed in searing white light. A white Rover squealed to a halt. A door was flung open, a shout. Magically, the two men bounded away, disappeared over a brick wall.

Lucy was left standing in the light, while a tall figure advanced and put his arms round her. At first Dr Roxburgh didn't speak to her at all. He held her in his arms rocking her to and fro, to and fro, like a child.

Then he put his fingers under her chin and tilted up her face. 'All right? They didn't hurt you?'

She shook her head and gave a faint uncertain smile. 'I'm all right.'

She found it difficult to talk. Her voice was croaky and her head spun. Part of her wanted to stay in his arms. Part of her wanted to escape the danger of them.

'Thank you,' she added belatedly.

'Thank heaven,' he said seriously.

'You were in the nick of time, as they say.' Lucy tried to laugh, and instead gave a strange little sound that was half a sob, half a feeble giggle.

'I was afraid this might happen.' He kept one arm round her shoulders and propelled her towards the car. '*Now* will you let me take you home?'

She shot him a rueful, apologetic glance which he correctly interpreted. 'Don't worry, I'm not going to lecture you. I ought to, but I won't.'

He helped her into the passenger-seat, then walked round and got in himself. Lucy sat for a moment, nervously clasping and unclasping her hands, her eyes downcast.

He turned towards her, cupped her face in his two hands and stared searchingly into her eyes. Unhurriedly, his mouth descended on hers, his lips moving slowly and sensuously. It was a strange, unfamiliar kiss, a hint of passion, more than a hint of rigidly suppressed desire, yet a sad kiss that demanded nothing. Her hands seemingly of their own volition rose to fasten round his neck, then fell back to her lap.

'You're trembling,' he said suddenly.

'I'm. . . I'm all right.'

'Were you very frightened?'

'I hadn't time to be.' I'm not trembling because I was frightened, she wanted to tell him. I'm trembling because I'm sitting here with you. I'm trembling at your touch. I'm trembling because you kissed me, because you kissed me *like that*. She couldn't have described how. Yes, perhaps she could. He had kissed her like someone who had perhaps once loved her—but no longer. Memories of those other, passionate kisses returned to trouble her.

'Where do you live?' he asked.

She heard the Rover start up smoothly and move forward. 'Three, Laburnum Villas. Just down the road on the left.' She laughed shakily. 'I was almost home.'

'Will anybody be there to look after you?'

'Oh, yes, Meg will be home. And Fenella.'

As he slowed down and brought the car to a halt outside Number Three, he lifted her hand. 'You've had a shock.'

She thought he was going to kiss her again, but his fingers slid to her wrist, found her pulse, paused.

He frowned. 'Rapid.'

Passion and memory were now a long, long way away. The clinician had taken over. She was a nurse he had rescued, a patient who had had a fright. 'Take care,' he said briefly.

He got out and opened up the passenger door, looking up thankfully at the reassuring lights of Number Three. She was their problem now.

'Tell them to give you a warm drink and put you to bed. I'd come up myself——' he thrust out his arm and looked at the watch on his wrist '——but I'm expecting a rather important call from the States.'

CHAPTER THREE

MEG and Andrew were deeply concerned about the attempted assault. They had been sitting at the kitchen table drinking cocoa when Lucy came in.

One glance at Lucy's face and Meg jumped to her feet. 'What on earth. . .?' She put her arm round Lucy's shoulder and Andrew pushed a chair forward for her to subside into. 'Sit yourself down, lass.' Then he hurried over to the stove to heat some more milk, throwing anxious glances over his shoulder.

'What happened?' Meg demanded.

Haltingly, Lucy told them. She managed to keep a tight hold on herself and maintain a steady tone of voice till she came to the part where Dr Roxburgh drove her home. Then her lips trembled and tears ran down her cheeks.

'There, there,' murmured Meg, patting her shoulder, 'get it out of your system.'

'There, there,' Andrew echoed, extracting the bottle of brandy from their small drinks cupboard. 'You get this down you.' He poured a generous measure and topped it up with hot milk, then handed her the beaker.

'I don't like spirits,' Lucy protested.

'Don't argue,' Andrew said mildly. But for some

reason those two echoing words sent her into floods of tears.

'Thank heaven for Dr Roxburgh,' said Meg, watching Lucy's face. 'I do wish he'd come in so that we could thank him in person.'

Lucy dried her eyes and said in a stony voice, 'He couldn't spare the time. He was expecting an important call from the States.'

'Oh.' Meg and Andrew exchanged meaning glances. 'Well,' Meg went on briskly, 'he'd done enough.'

'He'd done everything that had to be done,' Andrew echoed.

'What I can't understand,' said Meg, watching Lucy's face, 'is why you didn't let him drive you home in the first place. After all, there've been other incidents with suspicious characters round the hospital.'

'Dr Roxburgh's a very busy man,' Lucy told her.

'But not too busy to come looking for you.'

'I doubt he was doing that.'

'What, then?'

'He just happened along.'

Meg shook her head. 'I think he showed great concern—above the call of duty, as they say.' She stood up. 'Now let's be doing as he commanded. I'm going to run your bath. You can have some of my herbal oil—it's marvellous. Then off to bed with you. Things will look a whole lot better in the morning.'

The hot foamy water relaxed Lucy's limbs. She

could feel the tension being soothed out of her muscles. But her mind still squirrelled around over the events of the day.

She lay down for a while on her bed, staring up at the ceiling, where her mind inexorably projected disturbing scenes, all with Dr Roxburgh as the leading, dominating, half-desired, half-hated character.

She heard Meg and Andrew put on a tape and start dancing to it. Then, half an hour or so later, the sound of Andrew saying goodnight and the door slamming behind him. Then Meg humming as she tidied the kitchen and laid the table for the light breakfast they all tried to snatch before going on duty. In the end, she got up and put on her dressing-gown.

'Can't sleep?' Meg asked commiseratingly as Lucy appeared in the kitchen doorway. 'Do you want an aspirin? Or another hot drink? Or would you rather talk?'

'Talk, please.'

'Then sit yourself down.'

'Are you on early tomorrow?'

'No, praise be, late, so don't worry your head about me and my beauty sleep. Talk to your heart's content. Get it out of your system. Isn't that what your Charles would say?'

'He's not my Charles.'

'No?'

'No.'

'Would you like him to be?' Meg was in that

happy generous state when, having found the man in her life, she wanted all her friends to be just as happy and fulfilled.

'I don't think so.'

'Are you still carrying a torch for Dr Roxburgh?'

'No!' Lucy answered vehemently—much too vehemently.

Meg raised her brows and waggled them in humorous disbelief. 'I think you are. Maybe you even don't know it. Maybe you think you hate him. But it's like those tests your Charles gives—you know, those association tests. You've only to mention Dr Roxburgh's name, or something to do with him, and there's an instant reaction.'

'You're wrong,' Lucy protested.

'You don't see your face, love.' Meg rearranged the breakfast plates. 'I hope I'm wrong, I really do. And I'm only telling you this so you can get it out of your system. Get rid of whatever Dr Roxburgh has for you. Find someone who does love you. For there's nothing worse than loving someone when they love someone else.'

'You don't have to tell me that.' Lucy twisted her hands in her lap and stared down at them.

'Did he never mention. . .when you knew him before. . .that there was someone else?'

'To me? No, never.'

'Did he not mention that he was going to America?'

'Only when I already knew.' And in answer to Meg's questioning glance, 'I shared a room with a

girl called Nesta. She was a nurse on Dr Roxburgh's
team. She told me, because she thought I ought to
know.'

Lucy's voice trailed away.

'I know that sort of girl,' Meg murmured.

'What sort?'

'The sort who tells you what you ought to know.
But go on,' Meg urged her shrewdly. 'This needs
getting off your chest—more than the lout with the
broken bottle.'

'I think Nesta realised I was in love with him. But
after the arrival of Iris, this postgraduate researcher,
she knew. . .' Lucy's voice became husky, '. . .his
affections, as they say, had changed.'

'And all this she told you?' queried Meg.

'Oh, there was more. He'd asked me out to dinner
at Romano's in Cambridge. He was going to wine
me and dine me and then break the news and
farewell. You know, like giving someone a splendid
business-lunch and then the chop. In this case, "I'm
off to the States, and Iris is coming with me." Nesta
actually heard him discussing the arrangements with
Iris.'

'So?'

'So I didn't go to Romano's, of course. I couldn't.
I wasn't going to walk into that!'

'So what did you do?'

'Instead, I went to a party Nesta had fixed up.
Her brother had just qualified.'

'You knew him, did you? The brother?'

'Oh, yes,' said Lucy.

'Nice?'

'Very.'

'So you stood up Dr Roxburgh?' queried Meg.

'Oh, no, it wasn't like that at all. It certainly didn't seem like that at the time.'

'It wouldn't—it never does. And you had one helluva miserable evening.'

'Yes.'

'But you kept your pride?'

'Yes, I did.'

Meg twisted the new engagement ring round on her fingers for several seconds before saying in a low voice, 'Do you know, Lucy my dear girl,' her voice shook with unaccustomed earnestness, 'there's no such thing as pride in love. In real love.' She sniffed and almost visibly pulled herself out of her sentimental mood. 'Now here's me talking about love, when maybe you really want to talk about tonight and those rotten louts. . .get them off your chest. . .'

She was interrupted by the ringing of the front door bell. They both looked up at the clock on the kitchen wall. Ten past midnight. 'Fenella's forgotten her key again,' Meg said, shaking her head.

As she opened the front door, she began, 'How you ever remember your patients, I'll never know. . .' and then her voice changed. 'Oh, good evening, Sergeant. . .' and breathlessly, 'Dr Roxburgh! I thought it was our flatmate. Please do come in.'

Dr Roxburgh's eyes rested on Lucy's flushed face. He raised his brows. 'I told you to go to bed.'

'I did. But I couldn't sleep.'

'And I thought it best to let her talk about it,' Meg put in pacifically.

Dr Roxburgh studied Lucy's face. 'Do you want me to give you something?' he asked.

'No, thank you.'

The corners of his mouth turned down at her vehemence.

'This is Sergeant Sumner,' he introduced the thickset man in his thirties. 'I told him I hoped you'd be asleep, but as you're not do you feel able to answer a few questions? He's promised me he won't keep you long.'

'I'm fine,' mumbled Lucy.

In any case, Sergeant Sumner was already unbuttoning his top pocket and bringing out his notebook. Meg pulled forward a chair. 'Tea or coffee, Sergeant?'

'Tea, ma'am, if it's all the same to you.'

'Doctor?'

'Nothing, thank you.'

As they were sitting themselves round the kitchen table, there was the sound of a latchkey in the lock and Fenella came in.

'Nothing to worry about.' Dr Roxburgh got to his feet quickly, noticing her startled look at the assembled group. 'You might as well listen in on it, though.'

Meg moved her chair along to make room at the table. 'You can sit between me and the Sergeant.'

She smiled faintly. 'Sergeant Sumner, Fenella Jeffreys.'

'You remembered your key, then, ma'am?' He smiled teasingly as if to lighten the atmosphere.

'For once, yes.'

'You work at the hospital too?'

Fenella nodded. 'At physio.'

'I won't keep you long,' Sergeant Sumner said. 'The doctor's been very helpful and informative.'

When Sergeant Sumner had led Lucy through her story, he congratulated her on the clarity of her account. She was amazed that it should be so, for she had been aware that Dr Roxburgh's eyes had never left her face. But then it was comparatively easy to give a clear account of the attack, for she was not by nature a fearful person, and it had not been until she got into the car with Dr Roxburgh that she had been so terribly afraid.

CHAPTER FOUR

THE immediate consequences of the episode were that all female staff were issued with screamers, and Sergeant Sumner volunteered to give lessons in self-defence, to be held in the gym of the physiotherapy department, when it wasn't being used for Fenella's cardiac rehabilitation courses.

The most significant consequence as far as Lucy was concerned was that Dr Roxburgh's attitude to her became colder than ever, and she became ever more chary of close contact with him.

A hospital on the edge of a town became used to petty crime, and the incident, if not forgotten, was soon overtaken by other more important matters—possibilities of programme curtailments due to financial restraints, rumours of staff changes, talk of success and failure in the fertility unit.

Then, two weeks to the day after Dr Roxburgh's arrival, Lucy's bleeper summoned her to the telephone, as she locked up the drugs cupboard before finishing duty for the day and 'handing over the brick' to Staff Nurse Sillitoe.

She picked up the receiver in the corridor and announced herself.

'A very distressed lady,' Janet, the telephone

switchboard operator, told her. 'Wouldn't speak to anyone but you.'

Janet's tone warned her of what was to come. Anyone working in the fertility unit had to get used to a distress quite unlike anything they had encountered before. Patients regularly became hysterical with disappointment when they didn't conceive. Early on, medical staff learned only too well why hysteria was so-called. The Greeks were right: so often the seat of it was the womb. Added to that, hormone stimulation increased the propensity to over-reaction, and the very raising of hope made the consequent disappointment so much harder to bear.

Staff on the unit were told that whenever possible they should not leave a patient to deal with their distress alone. In the past, a woman had committed suicide in the distress of the moment, and there had been several attempts, happily unsuccessful.

As Lucy feared, it was Mrs Bowles. The insemination had been unsuccessful. Her period had begun. In between choking bouts of weeping, Mrs Bowles told Lucy, it wasn't just for herself, it was for her husband Ned.

'He'd been that chuffed at the idea of a little son.'

'Can I speak to Mr Bowles?' Lucy enquired. 'Is he with you now?'

'No. He's on long distance this week. . .'

'Will he be back tonight?'

'N-not till eleven.'

'Is there anyone who can stay with you till he comes?'

'No.' Through Mrs Bowles' hiccuping sobs, Lucy found out that the patient's mother lived up in Manchester, and her neighbour was on holiday. Her neighbour on the other side worked on the checkout at Tesco's and wouldn't be back till nearly nine.

'Listen to me,' Lucy said, making her mind up quickly. 'I'll come round.'

'But you won't be able to do anything if you do come round,' Mrs Bowles shrilled. 'What is there to be done? It's all useless! I'm finished with everything. I just want to give up. I don't want anyone troubled. . . I know nothing's going to do any good!'

'It's no trouble, Mrs Bowles, I know where you live,' Lucy told her. 'It isn't far. I want to come.'

'No, nothing's going to help now. I just wanted you to know. . . I'm going to. . .'

Suddenly there was a click and the line went dead.

'Janet,' Lucy requested urgently, 'please get that number back, will you?' She began to unbuckle the clasp of her belt, ready to slip into the dress she always kept in her cupboard.

'Sorry, Sister, but the number seems to be engaged.'

'Get the outside exchange to check, then. Find out if they're talking on the line.'

Lucy waited impatiently, biting her lip.

'Sorry, Sister, but Exchange says that number has left the receiver off. They're buzzing them, but they don't seem to be responding.'

Lucy stood for a moment, pressing her fingers to her forehead, while she collected her thoughts.

She felt a hand lightly touch her shoulder, and Charles Waters's soft voice asked quietly, 'Trouble?'

Lucy spun round and gave him a worried, rueful smile. 'Mrs Bowles, in great distress. And now she's hung up on me!'

Charles shook his head commiseratingly. He glanced at the clipboard under his arm, then twisted his wrist to look at his watch. 'Want me to run you there? I've no more appointments. I've one more phone call to make for this,' he tapped the clipboard, 'but it won't take a jiffy. Give me five minutes, then see you outside the front entrance.'

Eight minutes later, tucked in the passenger-seat of his old red MG roadster, Lucy thought the car was quite unlike the man. Charles was, as most people said, an enigma. He was quiet, and apparently undemanding, and his work seemed to be his life. He was a clever psychiatrist who knew how to draw other people out, but who revealed almost nothing of himself.

He dressed with quiet elegance, favouring silk shirts, yellow cravats, bespoke jackets and hand-made shoes. In the few weeks he had been dating her, she could not say she had got to know him any better. On the two theatre dates, and on a long walk by the riverbank, they had talked about hospital personalities, and his passion for psychiatry.

Each time he had kissed her goodnight gently, but without passion. Meg, who like to classify everyone, called him 'Still Waters', the assumption being that he ran deep. Maybe he did. 'There'll be hidden fires there, I bet,' Meg had once gone on to say, mixing her metaphors. 'He just needs the right woman to put the key in the door.'

'I'm sure you'll be able to help Mrs Bowles more than I will,' said Lucy, as with a roar of power, Charles accelerated the car away from under the hospital portico.

He turned to give her a wry smile. 'I doubt that. But thanks for the compliment.'

'I just hope she's all right,' Lucy worried, as the car turned into the thick traffic of Western Avenue.

Charles threw her a brief glance. 'She will be,' he said.

'I'm always worried a patient will. . .' She twisted her fingers.

'I know.' He took a hand off the wheel to cover hers. 'But she won't. I have confidence in our Mrs Bowles.'

With a frown of concentration, he stared at the traffic ahead. Lucy glanced at his profile, thinking inconsequentially of how pleasing it was—good forehead, straight nose, a curving sensitive mouth. How different from Dr Roxburgh's craggy, arrogant, unyielding face.

'I have confidence in her too,' she said. 'Up to a point. But. . .' She caught her breath with impatience as roadworks traffic lights brought the traffic ahead to a halt.

'Now don't get fidgety,' Charles said. 'It's the rush-hour. Everyone wants to get home.'

'I'm not getting fidgety,' Lucy lied, clasping and

unclasping her hands, till Charles took one hand off the wheel and put it steadyingly over hers.

'A great giveaway, hands,' he smiled wryly.

She sighed. 'I know.'

She watched his hands on the wheel, marvelling at his patience as he moved the car inexorably but unaggressively through every break in the traffic. Charles himself was a safe pair of hands, she thought. A woman could do worse than trust herself to them. And weren't safe hands better than passion that deluded you?

'Driving is a great giveaway too, isn't it?' she smiled. 'Don't they say you live like you drive?'

He nodded. 'Some of the pundits say that. Myself, I think you can acquire all sorts of surface calm and be very screwed up inside.'

Now he had a clear lane in the traffic and pressed his foot on the accelerator. The car leapt forward.

'At least you'll be able to explain to Mrs Bowles from a man's point of view,' Lucy told him, 'that her husband won't throw a fit.'

'The men don't, on the whole, I've found,' said Charles.

'Thank heavens!'

'But that doesn't mean they don't feel it just as much. Sometimes more.'

A strange note in his voice made her turn her head sharply and questioningly. She half anticipated he was going to say something more, but she must have been mistaken. His eyes were fixed on the road, his expression untroubled, but enigmatic.

'There's a short cut to Rowan Avenue at this next island, just after the Riverside Inn,' he said as if that was all that was engaging his mind. 'I'll have you there in two minutes flat.'

As they turned the corner into Rowan Avenue, Lucy began to dread what they would find at Number Forty-Seven. Might poor Mrs Bowles have taken an overdose, or simply rushed out into the gathering dusk towards the river?

When Charles rang the doorbell it seemed to echo with an ominous emptiness. There was no answer, so they walked round to the back of the semi-detached house. They hammered on the back door, but there was no answer.

A marmalade cat came up and rubbed itself against their legs and looked hopefully up at the back door. But no one came to open it. Back to the front door again. Lucy peered through the letterbox. Everything looked neat and ordinary, except that from the edge of the hall table the telephone receiver still hung at the end of its wire.

Charles crouched down beside Lucy and called, 'Mrs Bowles, are you at home?'

Nothing.

'It's no use going to the neighbours,' Lucy said. 'One's away on holiday, and the other is working.'

A further exploration of the house showed the curtains half drawn across an upstairs bedroom window, as if someone might be lying down. Or. . .

Lucy's mind was filled with that awful fear of a patient overdosing. She could almost see Mrs

Bowles up there and the empty bottle beside her bed.

Peering through the kitchen window, she could see no sign of any preparation for Mr Bowles's evening meal. But no sign of anything untoward either.

No, if there was any serious problem, it would be upstairs. When she turned round Charles's eyes were travelling from those half-drawn bedroom curtains to the small garden shed that stood amongst clumps of small fruit bushes. Against the hut was propped an old wooden ladder.

'Now don't panic,' Charles said, 'but I think I'll just take a look.'

'I am not panicking.' Lucy gritted her teeth.

He didn't bother to contradict her. Carefully he propped the ladder against the wall just below the bedroom window. 'If you'd hold the bottom steady, Lucy.' He began to climb cautiously. 'Not that I'm in any way anxious,' he threw over his shoulder.'

'Of course not,' Lucy said. 'Nor am I!'

She gripped the bottom of the ladder tightly. Hopeful of food, the marmalade cat was rubbing himself against the back of her legs and was now mewing hungrily.

The ladder creaked with every rung.

'Careful!' Lucy called up.

Then suddenly there was the sound of the front gate clicking, and footsteps down the path beside the house.

'Heavens above! What's going on?'

At Mrs Bowles's startled exclamation, Lucy relaxed her hold on the ladder and spun round. The ladder described a slow arc sideways, spinning Charles Waters headlong into a clump of currant bushes. There was a thud, an exclamation, the rustle and snap of leaves and branches.

'Oh, Doctor,' Mrs Bowles hurried forward, 'are you hurt?'

Then as she saw him get to his feet, fastidiously pulling out twigs from his hair, and brushing down his good jacket, the miracle happened.

Mrs Bowles's ravaged face broke first into smiles, then gulps, then into gales of irrepressible laughter.

'Come inside,' she managed to get out at last. 'Oh, I'm sorry to laugh like that! Please, let me help you tidy up. I'll sponge your jacket. Oh dear, there's a tear in it! I'll mend it. Are you sure you're not hurt? Oh, Doctor,' she touched his arm, 'you'll never know how much good you've done me!'

'I never thought today would see me laughing,' she said as the three of them sat round her kitchen table half an hour later. She warmed her hands round a mug of hot tea and stared down solemnly at its contents. 'I've run the gamut, as they say, from despair to this.' She turned to smile kindly and apologetically at Charles. 'But we've all had a laugh, haven't we?'

'We have, Mrs Bowles,' Charles agreed good-humouredly. 'I haven't laughed so much for a long time.'

Mrs Bowles hadn't asked what he was doing trying to peer in her bedroom window. In a way she explained why herself.

'After I'd rung you, Sister, I ran out of the house, and I honestly didn't know if I was ever going to come back. We all get so worked up, don't we?' She patted Lucy's hand. 'You staff have to take an awful lot of stick. I don't know how you cope with us and stay so calm. I'm sorry to worry you, dear, but it's so. . .important. . .and the disappointment is so awful.'

'I know.' Lucy squeezed her hand.

'I just walked on and on and then I found myself by the river. And you know, if you look at a river long enough, you do begin to think. . .well, why not? But I went on walking. I didn't let myself look at the river. Then I heard a clock chime and I thought, my goodness gracious, I haven't fed the cat, and so I came back home. Silly, isn't it?' Mrs Bowles began to laugh and cry at the same time. 'The things that bring you to your senses!'

The tears and laughter changed to pure laughter. A little hysterical perhaps, but pure healing laughter.

'Oh, dear, you in those blackcurrant bushes!' She drew in a deep breath and wiped the tears of laughter from her eyes. 'You've been good friends.' Mrs Bowles took a hand of each of them. Then she leaned sideways to whisper meaningly in Lucy's ear, 'You're well suited.'

Certainly Lucy felt a great warmth and trust in

Charles. He had been philosophical about the torn
jacket sleeve, the scuffing of his shoes, the stain on
his trousers. He had revealed himself as a kindly,
good-humoured and understanding man. Lucy
smiled across the table at him.

'You don't have to wait till Ned comes home. I'll
tell him myself—I'll explain. I'm calm about it now.
It'd be best like that.'

'If you're sure?' Lucy pushed back her chair.

'Oh, I'm sure! Now you've explained it all again,
it's all sunk in. And I'm sure of something else. I'm
not going to give up. No, sir! I'm going to try again,
and this time I'm going to make sure it's all right.
I'm going to put myself in Dr Roxburgh's hands!'

'So Roxburgh worked his magic on her,' Charles
remarked thoughtfully as they sipped a drink and
ate a home-made quiche at the popular Riverside
Inn on their way home.

They had suddenly remembered they hadn't eaten
since a snatched sandwich at lunchtime, and the
lights of the Riverside had beckoned them in. A log
fire burning in the snuggery had completed the
welcome.

'Mind you, it's not unusual,' Charles frowned,
'this fixation on the doctor. Especially in Fertility.'

'It's supposed to help,' Lucy pointed out, cutting
into her quiche.

'I think it does. But Roxburgh!' Charles pulled
down the corners of his mouth. 'Why not Duffey?
He's a good chap. And he did the insemination.'

'But unsuccessfully—or so it seemed to her,' Lucy pointed out.

'I'd sooner have Duffey.'

Lucy smiled. 'You're not a woman. Rupert Roxburgh exudes confidence.'

'And ambition. And arrogance.'

'You don't like him?'

'Frankly, no.' Charles watched her expression carefully. 'Do you?'

'Sometimes I do, sometimes I don't.'

'Mmm.' He smiled. 'That's typical female equivocation!'

'And that's a typical sexist remark if ever I've heard one!'

'Consider it struck off the records.' He dug his fork into his quiche and chewed a mouthful thoughtfully. 'Rumour has it you knew him before.'

'Slightly.'

'Enough to put you off? Or turn you on?'

'It was a long time ago. I've forgotten.'

'People don't always forget what happened a long time ago. Sometimes we go on carrying the scars.' Once again Charles seemed on the point of saying more.

'Do *you* carry scars?' Lucy prompted gently.

'Don't we all?' He frowned. 'Maybe even Dr Roxburgh.' He pushed his plate aside. 'I suppose if I'm fair, I resent him.'

'Why?' she asked.

'On two counts. Workwise, for his arrogance. And

no one can deny that. And on a personal count, because rumour has it he's after my apartment.'

Lucy looked surprised. 'That is a bit much.'

'Exactly my reaction.'

'The administrator won't give in to him, will he?'

'If it's for a good reason, he might,' he said.

'And is it?'

'He's senior to me,' Charles reminded her.

'That's not a good enough reason.'

'There's another. My flat is one of the larger ones—two bedrooms, a big lounge, intended for married staff.'

'But. . .'

'But he isn't. No, not at present. However, apparently his fiancée is coming over from the States.'

'Oh.' Lucy retreated into contemplation of her drink. Then she glanced up to ask, 'When?'

'When the lady in question's American contract is up. Three months, I imagine. Maybe more, maybe less.'

Lucy looked at her watch and picked up her handbag. She half rose from her seat. She wanted nothing so much as to get back to Three Laburnum Villas and go to bed—and forget all about Dr Roxburgh and his matrimonial plans.

'Don't go!' Charles put his hand over hers. 'Just when we're enjoying ourselves. Let's make an evening of it.'

Lucy smiled. 'I'm not exactly dressed for the occasion.' She pushed back her chair.

'You look lovely whatever you're dressed in,' he assured her.

'Thank you.' Lucy got determinedly to her feet. 'And thanks for all your help with Mrs Bowles. You couldn't have put on a better show if you'd specially designed it.'

'Oh, Mrs Bowles is my concern too.' He put his arm round her shoulders as they left the inn and crossed the car park. 'Though I can't always guarantee to fall off a ladder for my patients!'

He hugged her, and they both laughed.

Beside them, the reflections of the inn's multicoloured lights and the headlamps of cars on the bridge spun forward on the fast-flowing river that Mrs Bowles had hurried beside only a few agonising hours before.

'I feel we understand each other, Lucy. I feel we have a lot in common.'

He seemed more relaxed with her than he had ever been before—as if the episode with Mrs Bowles had drawn them suddenly close together.

Once inside the car, he put the key in the ignition, but didn't attempt to start the engine.

'You trust me, don't you, Lucy?' he asked suddenly.

'Oh, yes, of course!'

'Would you mind, then, if I asked you a personal question?'

'That depends on the question,' Lucy answered, wondering what was coming.

'Is there perhaps still something between you and Roxburgh?'

'No, definitely no! Why, has someone been gossiping?'

'In a hospital someone's always gossiping. But no, it's not that. Let's say it's my psychological observation.'

'Oh!' Lucy clasped her hands.

'To wit, every time his name is mentioned, you get defensive.'

'I don't mean to.'

'Of course you don't! But you can't hide all your feelings all the time. I don't want you to get hurt. You must realise he's not for you.'

'I do realise it.'

'So you feel quite free to have a relationship with someone else?'

'Yes.'

He put his arms round her and pulled her towards him. 'Prove it!' he said, and fastening his lips on hers, began kissing her with an almost angry passion.

She tried to draw away, but he held her tightly, even as another car swung into the park, its headlights spotlighting the two of them clasped together.

Lucy finally pulled herself away from him. They must have looked, she thought angrily, to the owner of the big white car that was now drawing up opposite them, like a pair of amorous teenagers.

Then she saw a middle-aged couple get out of the car—Lucy knew them, of course. They were the wealthy owners of the largest catering firm in the town, and were on the hospital's board of governors. They had just endowed an extension to Palmer Ward.

With them was Dr Roxburgh.

CHAPTER FIVE

PALMER WARD was situated on the first floor of the unit. It was small and homely and furnished as attractively as hospital funds would allow. Named after one of the pioneers of fertilisation techniques, it was known as the Three Rs—Relaxation, Reassurance and Remembering—remembering being one of the essential samples and tests.

It was here that patients were admitted after psychological counselling with Dr Waters or his assistant, Mrs Parsons, and after acceptance by the doctors. And it was here that Lucy, as sister-in-charge, had to help provide those Three Rs to some very apprehensive ladies.

The day after the incident outside the Riverside Inn, all she could remember was Dr Roxburgh's thunderstruck face. And as for Relaxation and Reassurance, she felt more in need of both than the sophisticated lady to whom she was explaining the treatment.

Sophie Spielman had just been admitted. She was an attractive-looking ex-actress in her late thirties, with long blonde hair and bold and restless eyes. She was married to a film producer, and off and on, she told Lucy, they had been trying to have a child.

'As you see,' Lucy explained to her, 'it's all very

informal. We've tried to make it as comfortable as possible, and as private, with the shutters between the beds. Your husband can visit you whenever he wishes between ten in the morning and eight-thirty at night. You'll have nothing more painful than some simple tests—taking your temperature regularly, taking samples to measure your hormone levels. And we must make sure you use your nasal spray.'

Sophie Spielman pulled down the corners of her scarlet mouth and sighed—but said nothing.

'Other than that, you can relax,' Lucy added. 'No smoking, of course. But the food's good, and there's television.'

Vera, the ward maid, was just taking round the trolley of lunches. Sophie wrinkled up her nose with distaste, as Vera swept the metal cover off a plate to disclose a savoury beef and onion stew and mashed potatoes.

'It looks revolting! And. . .' She swept her eyes over the other three occupants of the ward, at Mrs Minton-Smith, a lawyer's wife, genteelly spreading a napkin over her knee, at Kirsty Oates, a buxom farmer's wife already grasping her knife and fork, who looked as if the last thing she'd have difficulty doing would be producing young, to Isobel Caplin, a sad forty-year-old lady who had just won a court action to be impregnated with her dead husband's sperm. 'And. . .' Sophie dismissed them all with a toss of her yellow hair '. . .the whole ward looks revolting!'

'Come and sit beside me.' Kirsty Oates pulled out a chair at the central table. 'The stew's really good! You'll be nervous, lovey, like we all are.'

'I'm not in the slightest nervous! Nor am I hungry,' said Sophie haughtily.

'You've got to start eating for two.'

Sophie smoothed her hands over her flat stomach and scowled. 'Heaven forbid!' She turned to Lucy. 'So when does the torture begin?'

'It isn't torture. Treatment begins for you tomorrow. These other ladies are two or three days ahead of you. Tomorrow you'll begin with one tablet of clomiphene. That won't be difficult, will it? Now this is your little corner here, right at the end, near the television and the bookshelves. The shutters make it private for when you have visitors. And you don't have to go to bed till ten. Lights out ten-thirty.'

'Sounds like some damned prep school.'

'So it is—preparation,' Lucy said sharply, and left Sophie to undulate down the little ward. Grudgingly, Mrs Spielman took the chair between Kirsty Oates and Isobel Caplin.

She picked up the plate of lunch which had been left for her and inspected it more carefully. She had begun to eat by the time Lucy walked over to the desk to take the report flimsy which Andrew's assistant at the lab had just brought in.

'Is that my LH?' Mrs Minton-Smith asked timidly as Lucy stood studying the report.

LH stood for luteinising hormone, and though

Mrs Minton-Smith had forgotten what they stood for she knew the two initials stood large in importance in the life of the ward. LH and the other tests indicated when a patient should have the injection of ten units of hCG and be prepared for the laparoscopy.

'Yes,' Lucy came over and pressed Mrs Minton-Smith's thin shoulder, 'it looks as if you're at the next stage.'

'It is exactly like a damned prep school.' Sophie had clearly managed to pick up Lucy's pleased whisper.

'Doctor will write you up for the injection.'

'What will it be?'

'Something called hCG.'

'All those initials!' Mrs Minton-Smith sighed happily. 'What does it stand for?'

'Chorionic gonadotrophin.'

'Sounds dreadful!'

'It's immensely useful,' Lucy told her. 'It means we'll know when to perform the laparoscopy.'

'When?'

'Thirty-six hours afterwards.'

'Keep your fingers crossed for me,' begged Mrs Minton-Smith.

'I will.'

'Bless you! I've quite enjoyed it here. I'll be quite sorry to leave. Except. . .'

'Except that you're going on to better things.' Lucy smiled. She watched Mrs Minton-Smith attack her pudding with renewed appetite as Lucy began collecting the samples of the other patients. She had just rung for the porter to take them down to the lab, when a flamboyant giant with a mane of greying hair and wearing a long raccoon coat came striding into the ward, a long cheroot in one hand.

'Sophie Spielman, the actress!' he demanded with 'the' heavily underlined.

There could be little doubt about who he was. 'Your wife is at the far end of the ward,' Lucy told him. 'And would you please extinguish that cigar? Smoking's not allowed.'

'It's not a cigar,' he said.

'Whatever it is, I'll take it!'

She held out her hand authoritatively, and after a moment's hesitation he bowed to that authority.

But he was not done with her. 'How do you know I'm her husband?' he demanded.'

'I assumed.'

'Dangerous habit, assuming. I might well be,' he lowered his voice, 'the other man. Or are you too pure and touch-me-not-ish to know about other men?'

'Mrs Spielman,' Lucy repeated crisply, 'is at the far end. In fact, she's coming up to meet you.'

She turned, crushed out the offending cheroot and threw it in the rubbish bin.

'So I see.' He rushed down the ward, then stopped halfway down. In a theatrically ardent tone, he called, 'Darling!' and flung his great arms wide.

Like a young girl too long separated from her

lover, Sophie Spielman flew into them. The clinch continued, it seemed, for minutes on end.

'And what have they been doing with my poor pet?' He sniffed her hair. 'You smell of onions!'

'Onion stew. The whole place stinks of it. The food is ghastly!'

'Tell me about it.' With his arm round her shoulder, they departed for their little hidey-hole at the far end of the ward. 'I've brought you some things to cheer you up.'

Kirsty Oates put her head round the doorway of the sluice-room as Lucy measured up some more samples. 'My head's splitting! And I've got that rash again.'

'The drugs can have that effect, I'm afraid,' Lucy sympathised. 'Have a word with Dr Roxburgh. He'll probably write you up for something.'

'When?' asked Kirsty.

'Later on this afternoon, I hope.'

In the light of what followed hope was, of course, the wrong word. At that particular time, however, Lucy was just pleased that she could say his name so dispassionately and firmly. Her affection for Charles was beginning to help her dismiss Dr Roxburgh for ever.

'Well,' Kirsty said cheerfully, 'he's always a sight for sore eyes. How long before tea? I'm starving!'

Lucy turned to tell her half an hour, when she saw Rupert Roxburgh waiting outside. If he had heard Mrs Oates's complimentary remark, it didn't soften his expression. His face looked hard and cold and inimical.

'Convenient, Sister?' he asked, as if she had any choice in the matter.

'Of course.' She put up her hands nervously to her frilly cap as if to straighten it, and for some silly reason glanced in the polished side of the steriliser at her rather distorted reflection.

'You'll do,' Dr Roxburgh told her with ironic condescension, and stood back for her to precede him into the ward.

They both saw the sight at the same time. From behind the screen that separated the last bed from its neighbour rose a soft grey curl of smoke. The ward was filled with the aroma of an expensive cigar.

Mrs Oates, who was moving at her usual measured pace down the ward, turned to throw an agonised look in their direction, but Mrs Caplin again had her nose in a book and seemed oblivious.

Lucy let out an exclamation of apology and indignation. 'That man. . .!'

She hurried to keep up with Dr Roxburgh, her shoes squeaking on the polished floor. He had thrown her one exasperated glance, then set off to confront the miscreant.

As they rounded the screen Lucy saw to her horror that it was much much worse than she had supposed. There was not one miscreant but two.

Mr Spielman was puffing away at his cigar. And lounging with her beautiful legs crossed in the chair next to him was Sophie, smoking a black Turkish cigarette, her eyes dreamily half closed, her sulky mouth smiling.

The sight of Dr Roxburgh's face did not immediately intimidate her, but it certainly intimidated her husband. The large man seemed to collapse as if literally pricked.

'Sorry, sorry, sorry, a thousand sorries!' he said, pinching the cigar out with two fat fingers. 'Shall you be giving us a detention, sir? Or six of the best?'

'Both, if I had my way,' Dr Roxburgh said. 'But alas, hospital rules don't allow corporal punishment. Mrs Spielman, give your husband that cigarette to extinguish, please.'

Sulkily, she obeyed. 'And did you bring her in some cigarettes, Mr Spielman?' the doctor continued. They both hesitated, exchanged glances, decided to come clean and nodded. 'Very well, hand them back, Mrs Spielman. Or better still, throw them in the waste-paper basket.'

With a grand renunciatory gesture, Mrs Spielman tossed two packets into the waste-paper basket and looked up at Dr Roxburgh's face for some sign of approval.

She was disappointed. His expression remained dark.

'Smoking is not allowed,' he went on. 'For all sorts of reasons. But primarily, and overwhelmingly, for your own good.'

'I told you it was like a damned prep. . .' Sophie began, then met Dr Roxburgh's eyes and her voice trailed away.

In a studiedly even but deadly cutting tone, Dr Roxburgh enquired with icy politeness, 'Were you not warned that smoking was strictly forbidden?'

'Why, no!' they both chorused in unison, their mendacious eyes round with innocence. 'No, we didn't know. Honestly we didn't.'

'It's so relaxing,' Sophie added for good measure. 'So soothing.'

'So lethal,' Dr Roxburgh snapped. 'Especially for would-be mothers.'

'Sorry!' they both echoed again, and exchanged smiles like naughty children.

'Well, now you do know. I'd also like you to know something else. Should you not be prepared to abide by the rules of this unit, I'm not prepared to undertake your medical supervision.'

That threat appeared to crush them suitably.

'And now, Mr Spielman, if you would leave us a moment while I examine your wife?'

Dr Roxburgh did not as much as throw a glance in Lucy's direction as he carefully examined Mrs Spielman, and as he wrote up Mrs Minton-Smith for her hCG injection. Inside the small ward office, with the door closed behind them, dispassionately they discussed Mrs Oates's rash, and, with considerable concern, Mrs Caplin's manifest strain.

'Yet I see no alternative to Mark's decision to let her go ahead with the IVF attempt,' said the doctor. 'Do you, Sister?'

'No, I can't see an alternative. While there's even a remote chance she should be allowed to take it.'

'We can't work miracles,' he said. 'Though we can try.' His face momentarily softened.

But once the case-note file was snapped shut, the real Dr Roxburgh emerged again, and his ticking off of Lucy began.

It had lost nothing in the keeping. He folded his arms across his chest and frowned down at her from his formidable height.

'Sister, I'm astonished at your carelessness, at your lack of supervision. What's got into you, for heaven's sake? Your work used to be important to you. Why on earth didn't you warn them?'

Lucy stuck out her chin. 'I'm not answering that question.'

'Why not? Because you can't?'

'Because it's the wrong. . .' and picking up Mrs Spielman's vocabulary, '. . .the wrong damned question.'

'How dare you tell me what questions I should ask?' he demanded.

'Because you don't appear to have the perception to know.'

'Oh, I realise I'm not a psychiatrist!' There was heavy sarcastic emphasis on that word. 'But do tell me what I should have asked you?'

'Whether I did warn them or not.'

'And did you?'

Lucy was by this time almost too angry to reply. She paused for a moment, then gulped, 'Yes.'

'You don't seem so sure.'

'Well, I am.'

'I'm glad to hear it.'

'But you don't believe me,' said Lucy flatly.

'I didn't say that.'

'Not in so many words, no. But your face says it. You think I'm a liar, when you only have to look at those two to know they're. . .well, strangers to the truth.'

'I don't,' Dr Roxburgh said nastily, 'do quite such instant summings-up of people.'

'Well,' she said in a low voice that was wrung out of her, 'you don't have to do an instant summing-up of me, do you? You should know me better. You should know I'm truthful.'

'Should I? Should I indeed?' He took a step towards her and for a moment she thought that in sheer exasperation he was going to forget their roles and the formality of the situation, and actually lay hands on her and shake her. His face looked thunderous enough.

Then he held himself in check with an effort. 'I would have thought,' he said with deadly emphasis, 'the exact opposite pertained!'

For the rest of the afternoon that astonishing remark echoed in Lucy's ears. The injustice of it stung her painfully. It would have done from anyone. But the fact that the injustice was Rupert Roxburgh's overwhelmed her.

She would not allow him to get away with it. She hated lying, as well he knew. He appeared to have completely re-written her character. She would con-

front Dr Roxburgh. She was determined. Snatches
of dialogue she would have with him went through
her head as she handed over the ward log, the drugs
keys and the bleeper.

They still rang in her head as she made sure the
inmates of Palmer were happily settled, and her
imaginary conversation continued as she walked
thoughtfully along the corridor and rang for the lift.

The lighted arrow indicated that the next lift was
going up. But it stopped at the first floor and the
doors opened.

Only one person was inside. Dr Roxburgh was
keeping the doors open for her, and suddenly, for
all her imaginary conversations, he was the last
person in the world she wanted to confront.

She took a hasty step back. 'I'm going down.'

'Not just yet.' A hand reached out and pulled her
into the lift. 'I've got something to say to you.'

'When?' she murmured thickly.

'Oh, now's as good a time as any. We're both off.'

The doors closed and the lift continued upwards.

'There's a very good view from the top floor,' Dr
Roxburgh continued in the conversational tone of
someone showing round a stranger. 'Maybe Dr
Waters has shown it to you?'

'I've never been to the top floor,' Lucy told him.

'Then you're in for a treat.'

The lift stopped. The doors opened, and they
walked out into the long corridor that ran the length
of the whole building.

'There you are!' Dr Roxburgh pointed to the gold

cupola of the university, the curve of the river, the red-brick town with its jumble of streets and factories and warehouses nestling below. 'Wonderful view, eh?'

Luckily he did not appear to expect an answer. Just then she was not capable of giving one. Warily she watched him stop outside a white-painted door with the number two on it.

'This is mine.' He took a key from his pocket. 'Somewhat smaller than Charles's, which as you know is next door.'

She didn't know which flat was Charles's, but she said nothing.

'However, mine is really quite comfortable,' he added, like a stranger apologising for his somewhat humble pad. He opened the door and stepped back for her to enter.

The hospital was built round a central quadrangle, which Dr Roxburgh's sitting-room overlooked. Through the far window Lucy could see flower-beds full of red tulips and the small prunus tree in the centre of the lawn just coming into bloom.

She stared down at them. She didn't know exactly what he had brought her up here to say to her. What she did know was that she wasn't going to like it. Defensively, she tried to marshal all those thoughts and arguments that had been ringing in her head that afternoon. She had wanted to confront him. Well, here was her chance.

Yet such was his effect on her that she could think of none of them. All she could be aware of was him.

Even when she didn't look at him, had her back to him, in fact, she could still feel that powerful, frightening attraction.

'The bullfinches have already begun on the blossom,' he said conversationally, as he followed the direction of her eyes. And suddenly she remembered that walk with him through the flat sunlit cherry orchards four years ago near Cambridge. The fruit farmer bemoaning the bullfinches. How dared he remind her of those days?

'I suggest you sit down.' He waved her to an armchair. 'Can I offer you something to drink?'

'No, thanks.'

'Coffee?'

'No, thanks.' She perched on the edge of her chair. 'What was it you wanted to say?'

'First of all, don't sound so hostile. This is for your own good.'

'I feared it might be.'

'And the good of our team.' His voice hardened. 'Now I'm not going to talk to you as consultant to sister.'

'Thank you,' she murmured drily.

'More, let's say, like an old friend.'

Lucy almost covered her face with her hands. Everything he said made her dislike and resent him more. While every gesture he made, every raising of his brows, every curve of his lips, every spreading of his hands, made her ache for him to touch her and take her in his arms. She clasped her own hands and stared down at them.

'Look at me when I'm talking to you!' he snapped.
She looked up, scowling.

'Not like that. You remind me of Mrs Spielman.'

'You're not unlike Mr Spielman,' she retorted.

Dr Roxburgh gave a short, not unkind laugh.
Then his face resumed its forbidding expression.
'Really, Lucy, I've brought you here to help you.
You need guidance.'

'Personally or professionally?'

'Can one separate the two?'

He didn't seem to expect her to answer. She took
refuge in staring down at her clasped hands.

'I'm not going to go over this afternoon,' he told
her. 'I'm sure you warned the Spielmans. But you
have to watch patients like a hawk. People don't
always behave as they ought.'

'I know that,' she flashed bitterly.

Her anger sparked his.

'So do I,' he flashed back.

Then he controlled his anger. His expression set
into a kind of lofty sternness. 'No, what really
concerns me is. . .' for once the great man seemed
at a loss for words '. . .your behaviour. . .'

The statement caught her off guard. 'My behaviour?' she echoed. 'My behaviour when? How can
you possibly say that? What has it to do with you
anyway?'

'Cast your mind back. The car park at the
Riverside Inn. . .'

Lucy jumped to her feet. 'Oh, that!'

'Yes, that,' he repeated. 'It's hardly becoming for

two of the hospital governors, for two of the hospital benefactors, to see my nursing sister and the consultant psychiatrist in that situation.'

'That situation?' Lucy echoed, pacing up and down in indignation. 'You make it sound thoroughly improper. Do you know what that situation was?'

'I saw very clearly what the situation was. So did the governors.'

'I don't give a damn about what the governors saw!' Lucy flared. 'Do you know why we were there?'

'For the privacy of the car park, I presume.'

'Then you presume wrongly.'

'I'm glad to hear it.'

Loftily Lucy told him, 'We'd been to see Mrs Bowles.'

'Seeing Mrs Bowles doesn't mean you have to indulge in. . .that, afterwards.'

Just for one wild moment Lucy thought, He's really angry, and an improbable hope surged. Then she found that her indignant pacing had brought her to a side table. On it was a silver-framed photograph. It was of a beautiful smiling girl. The photograph was boldly inscribed 'To darling Rupert from Iris.'

Her anger was fuelled by an almost unbearable pain. 'Why shouldn't I?' she turned round and asked him. 'Why shouldn't I let Charles kiss me?'

'Not in a public place!' His unblinking grey eyes bored into her wide blue ones. 'You're a professional member of my team, and I expect you to behave like a professional, on and off duty.'

Suddenly Lucy was choked by a flood of emotion. No, he was right. One couldn't altogether separate personal and professional pain. The pain of the past, of what might have been, mixed with the day's doings, the row with and about the Spielmans, her continuing anxiety for Mrs Bowles, a sixth sense that told her the sad Mrs Caplin was turning dangerously inward to where no therapy could reach her. The hopes, fears, frustrations and sorrows of the past, present and future inhabitants of Palmer Ward pivoting on her own ability to exude Relaxation, Reassurance and Remembering were all undermined by this censorious lecture given by someone who had once said he loved her and understood and valued her, but who now no longer knew the first thing about her—yet who still held the power, at the touch of a hand, to melt her whole being into an unassuageable desire.

It was all too much! Too dangerous! Too ironic! Her face a flushed and furious red, tears welling in her eyes, Lucy stormed across the room and had opened the door by the time Dr Roxburgh caught her up and gripped her roughly by the left arm.

'And now you're behaving like a naughty child!'

She tried to pull away. 'Let me go!'

'Not till I've finished with you.'

'Let me go!' She had only one thought, and that was to escape.

Still struggling to free herself, she lifted her right

arm, swung it round and gave him a slap on the face that resounded round the apartment.

He stood stock still, looking down at her, his fingers biting hard into her left arm.

Then he said very slowly, 'There are times, Lucy, when I ache to put you over my knee and give you a good old-fashioned spanking!'

Her flush deepened to scarlet. 'And there are times, Dr Roxburgh,' she kept her voice steady, 'when I ache——'

'I'm sure, Sister! You've made that quite plain ever since I arrived. You argue, you contradict, you're antagonistic! I'm warning you, I demand loyalty on my team.'

Suddenly he let go her arm. He stood to one side. Then in words as cold as his eyes, he said, 'You either toe my line, or. . .' he opened the door wider '. . .you go!'

CHAPTER SIX

Lucy was still seething with fury when three days later the regular case conference was held as usual in her office.

She had positioned herself at the far end of the table, the furthest possible distance away from the chair in which Dr Roxburgh would be conducting the meeting when he came in.

'Good morning, Sister.'

'Good morning, Doctor.'

'I see I'm first.'

'Apart from me.'

Dr Roxburgh said nothing to that. He put down his files, sorted them into the order he wanted, then sat down in his chair. His cold, still hostile eyes regarded Lucy narrowly. Still smarting furiously under his strictures, she met his gaze squarely.

Charles and Mrs Parsons came in on the stroke of ten. Charles took the chair next to Lucy, with Mrs Parsons on his left. Then Meg breezed in breathlessly.

Last of all came Dr Duffey, late as usual, and sat down next to Lucy.

'Another garrulous patient, eh, Mark?' Dr Roxburgh asked sharply.

''Fraid so.'

'Very well, if you're sitting comfortably,' Dr Roxburgh opened his top file, 'we'll begin.'

He turned to Charles.

'Now, you counselled Mr and Mrs Bowles?' The cold eyes flickered over Charles's face. 'And in your opinion, they're both psychologically fit for another attempt?' His voice was as cold as his eyes. 'That right?'

'Yes.' Charles turned over the pages of his report folder. 'They're in a very positive state of mind. He's as keen as she is. The husbands aren't always, but he is.'

'And he's accepted my suggestion of the sperm mixture?'

'Yes. We talked it through.'

'And he'll be present?'

'Yes to that too.'

'You've established quite a relationship with the Bowleses?' asked Dr Roxburgh.

'A very good relationship, I'm happy to say, yes.'

'You and Sister visited, I understand?'

'Mrs Bowles was distraught. Lucy was justifiably anxious,' Charles told him.

'And subsequently continued the case conference at the Riverside?'

'Well, yes,' Charles looked discomfited. 'No law against that, is there?'

'No law, but some etiquette. A matter of taste and good judgement.'

Then, as if apparently unaware of Charles's suppressed anger, or Lucy's for that matter, Dr

Roxburgh continued with the progress reports. Mrs Spielman had decided she didn't want to go through with the programme. She wasn't sure now that she wanted a baby as much as all that. Mrs Caplin, Mrs Oates and Mrs Minton-Smith had had successful oocyte collection and implantations. Apart from Mrs Oates having to have the follicle flushed out, all had gone normally.

'I worry about Mrs Caplin,' Lucy said.

'We all do,' Charles put in shortly.

'Then get Social Services to follow up, Charles.'

'I'll try.'

'Do,' Dr Roxburgh told him sharply.

Charles flushed at his tone.

Mrs Parsons, gentle motherly peacemaker that she was, then asked permission to enquire from Dr Duffey how his patient Mrs Waddington was getting on—knowing, Lucy suspected, that this would lower the temperature of the meeting.

Mrs Waddington was to give birth, if all went well, to the unit's first test-tube baby. Her well-being was a subject of conversation, not only in the unit, but in the whole of the Hartington Hospital as well. A lady in her late thirties, who had tried for sixteen years to conceive, she had eight months ago been impregnated by Dr Duffey, using IVF treatment.

'She's fit and well, I'm glad to say,' Dr Duffey pronounced. 'Her GP is very happy with her. The scan shows a single baby, which she's pleased about. And there's no reason to suppose she'll go anything but full time.'

'I'll keep my fingers crossed,' Lucy said.

'If that makes you feel any better,' Dr Roxburgh told her. 'But it will certainly do Mrs Waddington no good.'

Dr Duffey smiled broadly as if Dr Roxburgh had made some witty joke. In the last week or so, Lucy noticed, he had become much less hostile to Dr Roxburgh—the renowned Roxburgh charm working its fabled magic, no doubt. Now it seemed to be only herself and Charles who were out of step with the new director.

There was a clue to Dr Duffey's changed relationship with his superior just before the end of the meeting. Dr Roxburgh was concluding his assessment of an American drug that reportedly had fewer side effects than clomiphene.

'We can still learn from our American cousins.' Dr Roxburgh turned then to Mark Duffey and added, 'As you'll shortly find out.'

No one but Lucy and Charles seemed to notice those few harmless words, because the next item was the purchase of a new hysteroscope. The relative merits of a Van Der Plas or the Hamou microhysteroscope were minutely discussed, the costs thereof to be raised by a garden fête and a fancy-dress dance.

The meeting finally broke up just before one.

'Come to the canteen and let me buy you a sandwich,' Charles suggested, putting his hand under Lucy's elbow.

And then, as they sat themselves down at a plastic-topped table by the canteen window, 'After this morning, I really do believe the latest buzz.'

Lucy took a bite out of her tuna sandwich as an excuse for saying nothing. She felt instinctively she wasn't going to like what she was going to be told.

'You heard what our revered chief said to Mark Duffey?'

'What about?'

'About America, of course.'

'Yes,' Lucy admitted resignedly, 'I did.'

'And what did you make of it?'

'I didn't know enough to make anything.'

'Oh, yes, you do.' Charles stirred his coffee and frowned. 'Dear old Duffey is being got rid of. He may be the first of many.'

Lucy looked across the table at him, wide-eyed. Dr Roxburgh's threat still rang in her ears. 'What makes you think that?' she asked.

'Several things. For one, Roxburgh's a new broom, and a prickly one, and, as he said that first day, he's got a big stick, which he intends to use. New brooms sweep very clean. Duffey was a contender for the throne, you know. He wanted the job.'

'But, with all due respect to Mark, he isn't forceful enough,' Lucy suggested.

'Granted. But new brooms don't like old contenders.'

They don't like old acquaintances either, Lucy thought, but not aloud.

'I always suspected,' Charles went on, 'that Mark would have to get on his bike.'

Lucy wanted to protest that Rupert Roxburgh wasn't like that, but she wasn't sure now what he was like. So instead she murmured mildly, 'I find that hard to believe.'

'Wait till I've finished. You'll believe me then.' Charles took a mouthful of coffee and wiped his lips. 'It's my certain belief that Mark's job is wanted for someone else.'

'Who?'

'Someone more congenial to our chief.'

'Oh, I don't think so, Charles.'

'Suit yourself, Lucy.'

'You're just going on hospital rumours.'

'Hospital rumours are very often true. I heard the rumour a couple of weeks ago that Roxburgh was encouraging Mark to go to America to get genned up. Now you heard what he said to him today. It's "America, here I come!" We also know he wants my flat—rumour says for someone from America. It's my opinion that a medico from Roxburgh's favourite hospital in Virginia is going to be swapped for Mark. It all fits in.'

'I don't see it's all necessarily connected,' said Lucy doubtfully.

'No smoke in a hospital, Lucy, without fire. The grapevine rarely gets it wrong.'

'I'm sure Dr Roxburgh wouldn't be as bad as that. I just can't see him getting rid of Mark, who's very popular, just so he can bring in a better man from the States.'

'Dear Lucy, who said it was a man?' Charles threw back his head and laughed. 'That's the *whole point*. According to the grapevine, it's a woman doctor. He's keen as mustard to have her over—on the phone to her every other day. A beautiful lady medico called Iris.'

Confirmation of the rumour came the following week, straight, as Meg would put it, from the horse's mouth.

From Dr Duffey himself.

He was, Lucy thought, just as innocent about the devious ways of Dr Roxburgh as she'd used to be herself. He appeared to be actually grateful to the man. 'I've been,' he said, 'as the chief pointed out, a bit of a stick-in-the-mud. Family circumstances. Mother's last illness. My marriage going phut.' He wrinkled his reddish brows, so that he looked more than ever like a well-loved teddy. 'But now it's time I flexed my medical muscles, as it were.' Dr Duffey stretched out his forearm to turn on the hot-water tap. His nice hazel eyes glowed with anticipatory pleasure. 'I can't wait to get to America. They're doing some fascinating research.'

'Really?'

'And I know,' Dr Duffey warmed to his subject, 'it's a good thing to have a woman doctor over here.'

'Yes, of course,' Lucy agreed.

'She worked at the Royal East Anglia for a very

short time—post-graduate research. You probably
didn't come across her. Iris Morton.'

'The name rings a vague bell,' Lucy replied steadily, not letting on by the blink of an eye how doleful
was that bell.

Dr Duffey scrubbed up with vigour, then shook
the water from his hands and unwittingly administered the *coup de grâce*, 'Dr Iris Morton-soon-to be-
Roxburgh.'

For the rest of the day that name threatened to
ring in her ears. Determinedly she put all thoughts
of Dr Roxburgh and his fiancée out of her mind.

Another name worried her with greater insistence.
Mrs Caplin.

Lucy walked through to her outer office and
opened the progress book where every phase of IVF
patients' progress was minutely recorded. She studied the entries. Mrs Caplin's period would have been
due several days ago. She had not rung for an ultra-
scan.

'Charles?' Lucy put her head round the door of
his office.

'Come in. Sit down.'

'I won't, thanks. I just wanted to know if you
organised a visit to Mrs Caplin?'

'As per our beloved chief's instructions? Yes,
indeed. A social worker is visiting tomorrow—first
available free time.'

'Thanks,' said Lucy.

'We don't usually visit unless the patient requests.
Shades of Mrs Bowles!'

'I know. But Mrs Caplin is specially vulnerable. A sad history—no husband, and an even greater than usual chance of failure.'

Charles spread his hands in helpless commiseration. 'We've done absolutely everything we can.'

'Thank you.' Lucy closed the door behind her. Then she walked back to the office, turned up Mrs Caplin's file and found her phone number.

At first she thought there was going to be no reply, then to her relief the line clicked open.

A voice said, 'Mrs Caplin's residence. Her housekeeper speaking.'

No, the housekeeper said, Mrs Caplin was not available. She was staying with her sister-in-law, her late husband's sister in Folkestone. Yes, she was in very good health and enjoying her little holiday. She had spoken to her earlier that afternoon. She was in remarkably good spirits.

Reassured, Lucy put down the receiver.

The following day Dr Roxburgh summoned her to his office.

'Sit down, Lucy.' He waved her to a chair.

His face was so set and hard that at first she thought he was about to bring up some further misdeed of hers for discussion. But instead he ran his hand through his thick black hair in a gesture of unusual distraction. He opened a newspaper and spread it in front of him.

'Mrs Caplin.' He tapped the newspaper. 'I've just been speaking to the police. She was found in her car at the foot of Beachy Head.'

'Dead?'

'I'm afraid so.'

Lucy wanted to cry out. She clenched her fists, gritted her teeth and forced her voice to be steady. But she could only manage one word. 'Suicide?'

'The police are treating it as an *accident*. There was no suicide note, no apparent sign of depression. Her sister-in-law said she was cheerful. The road conditions were slippery at the time.'

Lucy felt her eyes fill with tears that spilled down her cheeks. Dr Roxburgh dipped his hand into his pocket, brought out a handkerchief, and passed it wordlessly to her.

After a moment he said quite sharply, 'There's nothing we can do, Sister. We can only play a small part. We can't live other people's lives for them. This unit is not just a dream factory. There are nightmares too. There's life and death. Our patients have to be very tough. And to help them so do we.'

Then, as if to disallow any weakness, he pushed a list over to her. 'These are the names of new patients I'd like you to see—four of mine and two of Dr Duffey's. Confidentially—it hasn't been officially announced yet—he'll be running his number of patients down till his successor takes over.'

CHAPTER SEVEN

THE name of Dr Duffey's successor cropped up again the following week at Number Three, Laburnum Terrace.

The girls were giving a small dinner party as a belated celebration of Meg's and Andrew's engagement, and of course all the diners were interested in hospital doings.

At Meg's insistence, Lucy had invited Charles, and it was he who first mentioned Iris Morton-soon-to-be-Roxburgh.

'The would-be tenant of my flat,' he frowned.

'I hear she's a very clever doctor.' Meg shot Lucy an anxious glance, and piled some more potatoes on to Charles's plate to keep him occupied.

'Very clever all round, I'd say,' Charles murmured, before tackling the buttered, parsleyed feast with the gusto of a bachelor who usually cooked for himself.

'And is she really going to marry Dr Roxburgh?' Fenella asked the table at large. 'That's the buzz I heard.'

She who had declared herself a widow for life had invited Sergeant Bill Sumner, whose self-defence classes were now well established in Fenella's gym.

'I don't know,' answered Andrew. 'And I don't

think anyone else does either.' He began filling everyone's glasses with non-alcoholic wine because Sergeant Sumner would be going on duty later. 'You know hospital rumours.'

He sat down again and shrugged his shoulders.

'Usually nine-tenths true, I've found.' Charles swallowed up his last potato. 'I'd certainly take a bet on it.'

'Done!' Meg held out her hands for his plate.

'I'm serious,' Charles said.

'So am I.'

'I'm betting a bottle of champagne,' Charles said, 'that Roxburgh and Dr Iris will be married before Christmas!'

'And I'm betting they won't,' Meg contradicted stoutly. She got to her feet and began stacking up the dishes.

'We'll dance at their wedding! Just you see!'

Meg sniffed disbelievingly. 'Come and help me with the dishes, will you, Lucy?'

In the kitchen, Meg plonked down the dishes and put an arm round Lucy's shoulders. 'Don't let Charles upset you!'

'He doesn't,' Lucy assured her.

'Well, don't let the thought of Dr Iris upset you either.'

'Oh, I've got over that ages ago!'

Meg shook her head. 'I don't believe you. But it's nice to hear you say it. And we mustn't be too hard on Charles. He's a good chap; he'd make a marvellous husband. I know he's hard to get to know, he

never tells you much about himself, but one thing I
do know.'

'What?' asked Lucy.

'He's only rubbing it in about Dr Iris because he's
attracted to you himself.'

'I doubt that,' Lucy said soberly.

'He's in love with you,' Meg said firmly.

'No, he's not!' Lucy shook her head vehemently.
'I'm sure he's not. I can't describe it. . .'

She spread her hands helplessly. For how to
describe that certainty, that rapture of Rupert
Roxburgh's arms about her, of his body pressed
close and hers melting into his, of his lips on hers, of
his voice whispering in her ear, of her whole being
responding to him.

'. . .but I know when real love isn't there,' she
finished lamely. 'And anyway, it takes two people.
And I know I'm not in love with Charles.'

'Not yet,' Meg corrected. 'But there are all sorts
of ways of being in love, and love at first sight is only
one of them, and that's mostly for twenty-year-olds.
When you're a little older, love grows. It doesn't hit
you like a bolt of lightning. So you wait and see!'

She picked up a lemon meringue pie in one hand
and a chocolate mousse in the other. 'You bring the
fruit salad, Lucy.' Marching back into the dining-
room, she threw over her shoulder, 'And an open
mind and an open heart!'

Determined to take charge of the conversation
and keep off the subject of Dr Roxburgh and Dr
Iris, Meg now began talking vigorously about the

bonny baby competition at the forthcoming hospital fête. She and Matron were going to judge it, she announced.

But her efforts were not needed. Halfway through the demolishing of the sweets, the telephone rang.

'None of us is on call, thank goodness!' Meg smiled comfortably as she pushed back her chair and went over to answer it.

'Yes, it's me speaking,' she told the caller at the other end of the line. 'No, that's OK, we'd just about finished our meal.'

Then she listened intently, her expression changing. 'How frequent?' she asked after a moment. 'I see.' She paused and listened again. 'And Dr Roxburgh is already there? Good!' Another pause. Meg assumed her most tactful voice. 'Would you mind if I came along? Yes, I know you can cope—none better, believe me. Of course I know I don't have to, but this is unit history being made, and I'd like to come.'

She put down the receiver and announced dramatically to the room at large, 'Mrs Waddington has gone into labour!'

There was a moment's silence, then Charles said rather churlishly, 'So much for obstetric opinion that once impregnation has taken place the pregnancy should be the same as normal conception.'

'That's so,' Meg said. 'That's still true. The statistics are the same. Mrs Waddington's only a week or so prem—just caught us a bit on the hop.'

She marched off to her bedroom. Andrew pushed

aside his pudding plate and began gathering up the rest of the dishes. In a mixture of apprehension and high excitement, the party was over.

Lucy smiled affectionately at Andrew. 'Sorry your celebration ended so abruptly.'

'Och, not to worry!' Andrew grinned back. 'What better way to end it, if all goes well?'

When Meg re-emerged in her sister's uniform, Andrew said, 'I'll take you up on my bike.'

'No,' Bill Sumner put in firmly, 'that's my pleasure. I'll drop you off, Meg—travel in comfort. I've got to go soon. I'm on duty at eleven.'

Lucy glanced across expectantly at Charles, but he was swirling the last of his wine round in his glass and was staring into it, apparently bemused. He only seemed to return to the everyday world when, after a shy kiss on Fenella's forehead, Sergeant Sumner closed the door behind himself and Meg.

'I reckon I'll maybe bomb up to the hospital, and see how things are before I turn in,' said Andrew. 'The lads,' he jerked his head towards One, Laburnum Villas, 'will want a progress report from me. We all have a stake in this. We're all rooting for Mrs Waddington.'

When he'd gone, Lucy and Fenella scraped the half-eaten food off the plates and began washing up. Charles, somewhat reluctantly, picked up a cloth to dry the dishes.

'She'll be all right, our Mrs Waddington.' He slipped his arm round Lucy's waist. 'She's got what it takes.'

'And the baby too! I hope he or she is all right,' Lucy murmured.

'You worry too much. Just go on keeping your fingers crossed for them!' He kissed the nape of her neck.

'Dr Roxburgh's there,' Fenella reminded them, as if that was her particular brand of personal reassurance. 'I'm told that if anyone can deliver the baby safely if will be him.'

'Such touching loyalty!' Charles exclaimed drily.

'It happens to be an honest opinion.'

'So his fame has spread even to Cardiac Rehab?'

'Yes. You're lucky to have him at the unit.'

Then when the last dish was washed, Fenella untied her apron, hung it on the hook behind the door and said, 'Well, I'm off to bed. See you in the morning, Lucy.'

'Would you like a hot drink?' Lucy offered. For some reason she didn't want to be left alone with Charles. 'Hang on a moment, and I'll make you some cocoa.'

'No, but thanks all the same. I'm tired.'

'Me too,' Lucy sighed, subsiding on the sofa and kicking off her shoes, hoping Charles would take the hint. But he seemed unwilling to go.

'Mind if I put some music on?' he asked.

Lucy shook her head. 'So long as it doesn't disturb Fenella.'

'It won't, I promise.' He put in a tape of 'Last Summer's Love' turning the player down very low.

'Would you like a drink?' Lucy suggested with

grudging hospitality, adding pointedly, 'One for the road.'

'Only if you will. I'll mix us both one.'

'A very weak gin and tonic, then.'

'Very weak it shall be.' He went over to the sideboard. 'Ice and lemon?'

'Please.'

Charles returned with two clinking glasses.

'Cheers!' He raised his. 'Here's to this summer's love! Let's forget about last summer or any other!' He sat down beside her. 'Cheers!'

The drink tasted strong. After two mouthfuls, Lucy found her eyelids closing. Charles slipped his arm round her and pulled her head on to his shoulder. 'Make yourself comfortable.' His shoulder did in fact feel very comfortable.

'You're tired,' he said. 'Don't bother to talk. Just close your eyes—that's it.' He stroked the hair away from her temples with soothing fingers, then with his forefinger he gently touched her long eyelashes. 'They're like black silk fringes,' he whispered, kissing her ear.

After a few minutes, the warm room, the drink, the soft music, the rhythmic rise and fall of his chest had their effect. Lucy's own breathing became slow and deeper and she drifted off into a strange dream in which she was in Rupert Roxburgh's arms. She felt his mouth on hers, his body hard against her, his fingers unfastening the buttons of her blouse.

She snuggled contentedly closer.

Far away in the depths of her dream, she knew

she should, for some reason, escape. But she didn't want to. She wanted simply him.

As his fingers touched her breast, she gave a little moan of pleasure and fastened her arms round his neck like a noose, pulling his mouth down to hers. Her heart was pounding wildly—so wildly she opened her eyes. The dream dissolved.

It was Charles's neck her arms were round, Charles's face close to hers, Charles's mouth from which her lips were demanding such a passionate kiss. Charles's fingers sliding inexorably inside her blouse.

With an exclamation of pain and anger, she tried to pull away, but her exclamation seemed to be taken up by other voices.

The door from the hall had been flung open and in the doorway stood Meg with Dr Roxburgh behind her.

Without waiting for Meg's thanks, Dr Roxburgh turned on his heel.

In the silence they heard the front door slam and the angry start of his car engine.

'Well?' Charles got to his feet. He had the grace to look apologetic.

'Well what?' Meg asked sharply.

'What happened? Did we deliver a healthy baby?'

'Dr Roxburgh did, yes.'

'Boy or girl?'

'Boy,' said Meg. 'Both well—a little small but no major problems. In fact, it was wonderful. After all the efforts, a very moving experience. But now I'm off to bed. The hounds of the Press are already baying round the hospital, trampling over the flower beds, taking pictures. I'm afraid things aren't ever going to be the same again.'

'Things aren't the same the second time round, Doctor. This time I don't mind one little bit,' Mrs Bowles told Dr Roxburgh and Mr Bowles, as she lay, comparatively relaxed, in the lithotomy position, in the clinical investigation room. 'I'm not in the least afraid.'

In the adjoining preparation-room, Lucy unscrewed the top of a torpedo-shaped metal canister. Out rushed a cloud of curling steam. From amid the wraiths, she extracted a thin phial—the Donor X sperm. This she carefully mixed with Mr Bowles's sperm and filled the transfer catheter.

When she stepped back into the clinical investigation room Dr Roxburgh was sitting on a stool beside the patient. Briefly his eyes met Lucy's. Their expression was blank and distant, whatever anger he felt rigidly concealed.

With a curt motion of his head he indicated that Lucy should turn back the sheet.

'Don't watch me,' he bade Mrs Bowles with a gentle smile. 'Just turn a little more—splendid! Why don't you come nearer?' he called over his shoulder to Mr Bowles, who was trying to make himself look inconspicuous in a corner of the room, and immediately the big burly engine driver crept forward and gingerly patted his wife's hand. 'That's splendid. Well, you know what it feels like, my dear.' He smiled at Mrs Bowles. 'Was it uncomfortable last time?'

'Only a bit.'

'Well, it'll be only a bit this time.' He held out his right hand without looking at Lucy and she put the transfer catheter into it.

'Right, Mrs Bowles.' There was a moment's pause, and Lucy held her breath. It always seemed very solemn, very momentous. Mrs Bowles gave a little gasp.

Then Dr Roxburgh said, 'That's it, Mrs Bowles! It's all done. Sorry about the cramps. But just think it's going to be a beautiful baby—a big strong healthy baby.'

'A second Ned,' muttered Mrs Bowles, turning her eyes towards her husband, her voice half excited, half tearful.

'Prime Minister Edward Bowles,' Dr Roxburgh smiled, patting the patient's hand. 'There now, Sister will look after you.' He handed the catheter back to Lucy and stood up.

'I couldn't be in better hands,' Mrs Bowles smiled. 'She's lovely, isn't she?' She gazed fondly at Lucy.

'I believe that's the general opinion,' Dr Roxburgh replied shortly. It was clearly not his.

'And how's the test-tube baby?' Mrs Bowles asked him.

'Doing splendidly.'

'What are they calling him?'

Dr Roxburgh for a moment looked discomfited. A slight flush crept up under his tan. 'I'm embarrassed to say,' he gave Mrs Bowles a wry smile that did not encompass Lucy in its beguiling warmth, 'they're calling him Rupert.'

'After you? Oh, that's wonderful! Quite right. Isn't that so, Sister?'

'Absolutely,' Lucy agreed.

'Let's hope he takes after you in character as well as in name,' Mrs Bowles continued.

Lucy raised her brows, and for the baby's sake countermanded that hope.

'Oh,' Dr Roxburgh smiled, 'the parents will probably change their minds before the christening. People change, don't they, Sister?' His smile faded, his mouth hardened.

'Out of all recognition,' Lucy agreed coolly.

She watched him drop his mask and gloves into the disposal bin, and turn on the taps above the washbasin.

Mr Bowles had straddled the stool Dr Roxburgh had vacated and was talking earnestly to his wife. They were out of earshot.

As he scrubbed his fingers ferociously, Dr Roxburgh demanded in a low voice, 'What exactly is going on between you and Charles Waters?'

'What do you mean?' queried Lucy.

'You know perfectly well what I mean.'

'If it's what I think you mean, that's our own business,' she said coldly.

'Do you love him? Are you having an affair with him?'

'I refuse to answer that.'

'I think you already have,' he replied grittily, and walked out.

Mr Bowles stayed with his wife, talking to her, holding both her hands in one large one of his and gently stroking back her hair with the other, every now and again whispering something in her ear that made her smile, while Lucy raised the blinds and tidied away in the preparation-room.

She longed for the insemination to be a success for the Bowleses. They would make excellent parents. That was how a marriage should be, Lucy thought. If a baby were conceived, it truly would be conceived in love. Professionally too, she was curious to see if the mixture of sperm as advocated by Dr Roxburgh would succeed.

When the half-hour rest period was up, Mrs Bowles lay with her hands on her stomach. 'Congratulate me,' she told Lucy. 'I'm pregnant—I just know I am.'

'Good for you!' Lucy smiled. 'But wait and see.'

'Your nice friend sister Meg has asked me to come and help with the bonny baby competition at the fête. Ned's going to run the bouncing castle. We feel part of the hospital family. Shall I dress now?'

'Yes, do.'

Lucy was still standing by the window, gazing out, when Mrs Bowles returned to say goodbye. She was watching a white-coated figure, Dr Roxburgh, his black hair ruffled in the wind, the corners of his coat flapping as he took a short cut across the lawn to the lab block.

'Well, Sister,' said Mrs Bowles, 'Keep your fingers crossed for me. We'll see you at the fête.' For a moment her bright, curious eyes travelled from Lucy's face to the white-coated figure who was the object of her gaze. She squeezed Lucy's arm and winked. 'And I'll really keep my fingers crossed for *you too*, Sister!'

CHAPTER EIGHT

THE morning of the fête was overcast, but by lunchtime the clouds had cleared away and the sun emerged. The national Press, who had had a field day reporting the first test-tube baby at the Hartington, had gone back to London and everything on the surface had settled down to normal.

By one o'clock the stalls were up on the playing field in front of the hospital, where occasionally a scratch team of medical staff took on the local cricket or rugby team. The inflatable castle was in pride of place, and Ned Bowles in his railway uniform had stationed himself at the ticket booth. An army of amateur cooks had brought in cakes and pastries and jams. A posse of ladies was sorting boxes of toys and jumble and white elephants.

Having declared the fête open, the chairman of governors went round every stall with Dr Roxburgh, the appeals secretary and Matron in attendance. Years ago, the governors had voted unanimously to retain a matron, when other hospitals were handing the running of the hospitals over to administrative officers. It was a wise decision. Matron Madison was a large lady with fine bold brown eyes and the opulent voice of a diva. She was respected not only in the hospital but in the surrounding town.

She made straight for the bonny baby competition where Meg and Lucy had set up a table under an awning, with basket chairs and a set of scales and baby-changing facilities in a little tent at the rear.

Mrs Bowles had arrived, and shook Matron's hand.

'You're not competing today?' Matron trumpeted.

'No, but this time next year. Fingers crossed!'

Mrs Bowles pressed her stomach. The second day of her period had come and gone—a fact that had already been entered with cautious optimism in the book at the unit. Mrs Bowles was jubilant, still beaming as she watched Matron sail away to the bric-à-brac stall.

Meg, busy weighing the first entrants—two identical girl twins—sounded a cautionary note. Too many optimistic entries in the book had come to naught. 'Wait a while yet and see,' she advised.

But Dr Roxburgh had sauntered over, looking very casual and approachable in blue denims and crisp white open-necked shirt. Meg appealed to him.

'On the whole,' he replied diplomatically, 'I'd usually trust a woman's instinct.' For a moment his eyes rested on Lucy's face. 'Women have a certain sixth sense.'

Lucy's sixth sense told her he was turning over in his mind whether or not to tell her something—something rather important to him.

'That's why,' he went on, the decision apparently taken, 'we're so fortunate to have persuaded a former colleague of mine, a very clever lady——'

'Did she need much persuading?' Lucy heard a voice that must have been hers ask harshly.

Dr Roxburgh smiled with a typically male satisfaction. 'No, not really. It. . .er. . .suited Iris very well.'

Meg tucked up the twins in their carrycot again, and, alarmed at Lucy's bleak expression and her frozen silence, asked, 'Is this the Dr Iris Morton we've heard so much about?'

'I didn't know it was common knowledge, but yes, I presume so. She's only young, but she's established a brilliant reputation.'

'The Dr Morton-soon-to-be-Roxburgh?' Lucy asked in a strangled voice.

Dr Roxburgh had the grace to flush. 'I'd no idea that was known too.' He shook his head in good-humoured disbelief. 'My goodness, how things get around in a hospital!' And, trying to laugh it off, 'Is nothing sacred?'

'And is it true?' Lucy breathed with the painful determination of someone cauterising a wound.

'Well, yes.' He raised his eyebrows in that half-humorous, half-deprecating, once wholly beguiling manner. 'The last I heard from her it was.'

'From Dr Morton?'

'Yes.' He gave a thin smile. 'But women have a habit of changing their minds. However, so far so good. I don't think she's going to wriggle out of it this time.'

Then, as if totally unaware of the devastation he was leaving behind, he turned to admire the next baby in the queue and congratulate the young mother on such a splendid little fellow.

The afternoon wore on. 'Is Charles making an appearance?' Meg enquired.

Lucy shook her head and smiled. 'He volunteered for duty. Mrs Parsons wanted to come. He said garden fêtes and bonny babies are not for him.'

'Wait till he's a father himself,' Meg grinned, and winked meaningly. 'Just you wait!'

In between examining babies and popping them on the scales, Lucy watched the kaleidoscope of people, old and young, all it seemed, carrying boxes of goodies or house plants, or if they were children, carrying toys. Faces swam into her consciousness, an old lady beaming with her arms full of fresh picked flowers, a boy carrying a handmade wooden engine, a spiky-yellow-haired teenager with tears in her eyes, which she wiped away with the back of her hand. Why tears? Lucy wanted to ask her.

Then Ned next to them on the bouncing castle, shouting at a youngster who had knocked his brother over, attracted her attention. When she looked again, the girl had melted into the crowd. Now Ned was chatting to the boy who had just bought the wooden engine, telling him he drove one very like that. A young couple hurried by, arguing vociferously. A little girl fell over and began screaming, and Lucy rushed forward to pick her up.

'It's all life here, isn't it?' Meg smiled. Then she looked at her watch and whistled. 'Three-thirty—duty calls. Must love you and leave you. I've made a list of the entrants and given them all marks. So far the twins are leading on my marking system, but it will be Matron and Dr Roxburgh who have the final say-so. Babies and judges should all be back by four.'

She then left to return to her maternity ward for the early evening shift, and all was well and all was normal then.

Four o'clock, and Matron arrived at the bonny baby stall at precisely the same second, Dr Roxburgh a few minutes later with a couple of children in tow belonging to his registrar obstetrics. He was good with children, Lucy noticed with wry sadness. He attracted children. They trusted him. He would make a good father to Iris's children.

Lucy presented the score cards to Matron and to Dr Roxburgh, and after they had conferred for a few moments, and patted the cheeks of the contestants and admired their sturdy limbs and contented smiles, the twins were unanimously declared the joint winners.

It was a popular win. The proud father, the baker, Mr Yates, took reels of photographs. So did the local Press. A silver cup tied with pink ribbons and a gigantic pack of baby toiletries were presented. There were second, third and fourth prizes and every baby was given a rattle, and admired. Every baby was a winner, every baby a miracle, Dr Roxburgh told them, and the crowd applauded.

The bonny baby stall seemed to be besieged by enthusiastic well-wishers. The Hartington was becoming a centre of excellence in the south, and its community was proud of it.

Dr Roxburgh told the crowd that efforts such as these would make more research possible. They were buying new equipment. They were exchanging ideas with medical men and women all over the world, especially in America. Lucy studied his face as he spoke. It was the face of a man devotedly in love with his job and with the woman who was to share it.

Lucy sighed. The afternoon had become oppressive and threatening. A sneaky wind had blown up, and thunderclouds darkened the distant city horizon. A splash of rain plopped heavily on the plastic awning.

Mrs Bowles, with a 'Sure you don't mind if I pop over to get a cake for Ned's tea before they shut up shop?' had left for the attractions of the home-made produce stall.

In her place came Mr Bowles. He was well pleased with his takings on the inflatable castle. He set about taking down the awning, folding the trestle-tables, carting away the weighing machine, and boxes of discarded rubbish. Then he went off in search of his wife. That just left the remnants of the makeshift nappy changing area to tidy away.

Lucy grabbed a large black dustbin bag and began emptying the overflowing nappy bins. She tidied away the little plastic folding table and scooped up the paper sheets and towels and stuffed them away. Her hand was just reaching for a large discarded cardboard box when she saw something in it move and heard a faint indescribable noise.

Her first thought was that it was the sound of raindrops on plastic, then that it was a rat, and instinctively she drew back. Rats and mice were a perennial problem round anywhere where there was food, and even a well-run hospital was no exception.

But she forced herself forward—and then she saw a tiny purple fist, a bundle wrapped in a torn blanket and a fragile little head, ominously blue.

Even before she saw the note pinned to the blanket, she had picked up the baby, held it close and protectively to her and run. Like a mad thing, she ran across the trampled grass, shouting her need for help—help to get the baby to Intensive Care without delay. Rain, quite heavy now, was falling on her head and running down her face, and splashing on the little blue head which she tried to crouch over and shield.

Then someone else was running faster and stronger beside her. She was aware that Rupert Roxburgh had taken the baby from her, that doors were flung open. As in a nightmare they seemed to be running down miles of corridor, round endless corners, through endless doors. Her mind was full of flickering unfocused images as in a broken cinema projection.

Reaching Intensive Care was like reaching some white-tiled, polished-steel heaven. The staff swung into action and the real fight began.

* * *

Three hours later, the colour of Little Boy Blue, as Dr Roxburgh had christened him, was better, his heartbeat stronger, his breathing less shallow. But there were still, he feared, going to be serious long-term problems.

The note pinned to Little Boy Blue's blanket had been deciphered. In an unhappy scrawl, it said,

> Please find a good home for him. I can't look after him. He's three weeks old. I haven't got a name for him. I think he's poorly.

With a dangerous sense of intimacy, Lucy and Dr Roxburgh had shared a tray of coffee and sandwiches that the IC sister had ordered for them. Another dangerous feeling, the euphoria of a young life saved, enfolded them.

The stormy relationship of the last few weeks was forgotten. It wasn't so much that Lucy thought to herself, If only things could have been different. It was as if indeed things were different—totally different. They existed on another plane, another planet.

Darkness had fallen and the rain had stopped when together they left Intensive Care and went through the main hospital entrance out into the drive. The air was full of the smell of crushed grass, and of earth after rain.

A small crescent moon had risen above the dark outline of the trees. Without words being spoken and without the need for words, their feet, seemingly of their own volition, left the drive and crossed the moist patchy lawn. Their feet paused in the shadow of an oak tree. The distant hum of the city served only to encapsulate their own quiet. They were the only two people in the world.

Dr Roxburgh took Lucy in his arms as if it were the most natural thing to do. His mouth pressed hard and passionately on hers, and with a joyful leap of her heart her whole being responded. Her body ached for the touch of his fingers, which travelled now down her spine, now caressing her breast. Momentarily, she felt dazed by her own desire, weak with her own compliance.

Then reality abruptly reasserted itself. Her mind threw off the excitements and euphoria of the last few hours, and memory flooded back. She remembered what Dr Roxburgh had more or less announced that afternoon. She remembered Dr Iris Morton-soon-to-be-Roxburgh and struggled in his faithless arms. Her struggles only inflamed him. She backed a step, but found herself trapped by the trunk of the tree, his body hard against hers. She was frightened of the apparent intensity of his feelings, but far more frightened of her own.

Then to help her at that moment came the thought of how little he must respect her. Knowing now that it was common hospital knowledge he was to marry Iris, he still thought he could twist her round his little finger, amuse himself with her till Iris arrived, as he had amused himself with her all those years ago. Frantically she moved her head sideways, trying to free her mouth. But when he released her lips it was to say in a low vibrant, exultant voice, 'You love me, don't you? I know you love me, Lucy.'

She knew too, but only something final and devastating could save what remained of her pride. 'Of course I don't love you. I despise you.' She paused, breathless, her heart thundering. 'You were right— I do love someone else.'

He stared at her for a moment in total disbelief. Then her words seemed to penetrate.

After that the effect was immediate. His hands dropped to his sides and he backed away. Suddenly Lucy felt icy cold.

The news of the finding of Little Boy Blue received much less attention in the Press than the homegoing of the Hartington Hospital's first test-tube baby.

'Be careful,' Dr Roxburgh told his staff. 'The intrusion of the Press has the power to change lives.'

That did in fact prove to be the case.

Fortunately, Lucy was on duty when the television camera crew was at work outside the hospital main entrance. But Mark Duffey, Charles Waters and Mrs Parsons were screened with the happy family group as it left for home. Their photographs appeared in some half a dozen newspapers with the caption THE WINNING TEAM.

The television pictures were distributed countrywide and had some unexpected results. Voluntary subscriptions poured in. 'Enough,' as Dr Roxburgh said, 'for several hysteroscopes.'

Gifts of baby clothes arrived by the score. Generous in their happiness, Mr and Mrs Waddington donated most of the clothes and equipment to Little Boy Blue, who now had a layette and cot and pram fit for a prince. But no sign of his mother or any relative who wanted him.

Frail and small though he was, he was already possessed of a definite personality. His big blue eyes followed everything that went on in the nursery. Despite his physical condition, he made little happy chortling sounds, and he rarely cried. His head had grown a faint blond fuzz of fine hair, and one of the cleaning ladies said she feared for him. He wasn't going to stay long in this world. Already he looked too much like a little angel.

Little Boy Blue's future was discussed in more practical terms at the next case meeting. Dr Roxburgh was having more tests run on him. There was something more that he needed to get to the bottom of. Meanwhile the police would continue their search for the parents.

'You can tell us more on that, Mrs Parsons.'

'We've asked the Press to publicise. We've had leaflets handed out. The social workers are helping all they can. And we've made three radio appeals.'

'It has never ceased to amaze me,' said Charles, 'that the world seems full of people desperate to have babies, or people desperate to get rid of the babies they've got.'

'That's simply a sweeping generalisation,' Dr Roxburgh told him crisply, 'and adds nothing to the discussion.'

Lucy and Mrs Parsons exchanged glances. It was becoming increasingly clear that the antipathy between Dr Roxburgh and Charles was deepening. Charles obviously felt threatened, and Dr Roxburgh, perhaps because of the stress of his job and his impending marriage, seemed to have a very short fuse.

'Can either of you remember,' Dr Roxburgh's eyes travelled from Meg to Lucy, 'being at any time suspicious of a woman with a baby?'

'It might have been a man,' Charles suggested. 'The father.'

'Possibly, but I don't think so. Well?' Dr Roxburgh looked at the two girls again.

Meg replied, 'There were thirty-eight mothers who entered their babies. You know me, Doctor, I chatted to most of them. But no one I could say I was suspicious of. They were a lovely lot.'

'Sister?' He turned his eyes to Lucy.

'No, no one suspicious. Lots of people were buying things and walking round with boxes.'

'Could she have got into the changing tent without going past you?'

'Oh, yes. It was open from both sides for safety. Mothers were in and out all the time, even when they weren't competing.' She paused. 'It's probably not worth mentioning, but I saw a young girl crying.'

'Was she carrying anything?'

'No.'

'Probably quarrelled with her boyfriend,' Charles said.

Dr Roxburgh addressed Mrs Parsons again. 'If the parents can't be found he'll be in council care till adoption can be arranged.'

'Yes, there'll be no difficulty there. I'll get our social worker on to it. There's a waiting list a mile long of would-be adoptive parents. That, of course, is providing he's fit and well. Adoption would be much more difficult if he's not.'

'That's going to be the sixty-four-thousand-dollar question.' Then for a moment, Dr Roxburgh's eyes rested on Lucy. 'You acted very promptly, Sister,' he said with lofty detachment, as if those memorable few minutes in the darkness of the garden had never taken place.

Lucy was too choked to say anything. She shrugged dismissingly. Charles, sitting next to her as usual, put his arm round her shoulders, gave her a brief hug and said, 'Well done, darling!'

He smiled challengingly across the table to Dr Roxburgh. The consultant met his eyes coldly and quellingly, and Charles had to lower his before Dr Roxburgh opened the patient progress file.

Lucy forced herself to listen to his prognosis of two patients treated for ovarian adhesions by the newly acquired video-laseroscope. Then on to Mrs Armitage. She had missed her period, giving rise to considerable hope, but the ultra-scan had proved negative, so it was the final failure for her. Mrs Bowles, however, was positive.

At that point, Charles's bleeper sounded. The

telephone exchange had an urgent incoming call for him.

'Mind if I use your telephone, Lucy, dear?' he asked.

'Of course not.'

'Sorry to interrupt the meeting, Rupert,' Charles apologised.

'No matter—I'd just about finished. Except to announce officially that Mark has secured an appointment at the Henrico. He'll be there for six months. I think we should all congratulate him,' said Dr Roxburgh.

Everyone in the group smiled and gave a token clap.

'And to tell you that Dr Morton, as some of you already know, will be coming in his place. I'm sure you'll all welcome her.'

As they all got to their feet, Charles—still waiting for the call to be put through—put his hand over the receiver. 'It'll be the usual lady in distress, I fear.'

He smiled at Lucy and perhaps for Dr Roxburgh's benefit made it a smile of special tenderness.

But the caller when she was put through, though a lady, did not appear to be in any distress. She seemed to be calling from a long way away, and it was as if she was trying to pitch her voice across vast distances.

'Charles! Charles! *Darling Charles*!' The voice was clearly audible to the whole room. 'It's *me*! It's Tamsin! Really it *is*! I saw you on the television, outside your hospital. It's me,' she repeated. 'Can't you hear?'

For a few seconds the case conference members stood rooted in embarrassment.

Not so Dr Roxburgh. Brusquely he shepherded them all, including Lucy, outside.

Lucy walked down the corridor with Meg, aware that her friend was eyeing her sympathetically to see how she was taking this latest development. Then as Meg turned left to go up on the escalator to Maternity, Lucy popped into her clinical investigation room to make sure all was ready for afternoon surgery.

By the time she returned to her office, it was empty. A note was scribbled on her desk pad.

Sorry about the call. I've just had a ten-thousand-volt shock! Don't know if it's good, bad, or just lethal! Will you come up and have a drink at the flat this evening? Say seven.

Charles.

CHAPTER NINE

IT WAS nearly half-past seven before Lucy could leave work. Before that, she had to take part in two counselling sessions, one, with Mrs Parsons, of a single lady who was considering having herself impregnated by donor sperm and who wanted purely female advice. The other was of a couple, who had been referred by their GP for IVF. The session began at six and was with Dr Roxburgh.

It was held in Dr Roxburgh's office. A tray of coffee and biscuits was ready on a low table, and four club chairs arranged round it.

Dr Roxburgh was standing by the window, studying a folder of Mr and Mrs Quinn's referral notes. 'I'll lead them through the medical details first, Sister,' he said, 'then they can ask you anything I haven't covered.'

Though he eyed her probingly, his voice was studiedly neutral and businesslike. It was impossible to gauge what his memory was of those few perilous minutes in the garden, if indeed he had any particular memory of them at all.

'They also might like to have a few words with you alone afterwards. They might feel less restricted than with me.'

He raised his brows, not without wry humour,

inviting her, almost daring her to comment, but Lucy wisely kept silent.

The Quinns arrived punctually, and, like all other new patients in the unit, were nervous, and ready to be embarrassed. Dr Roxburgh at once set about putting them at their ease. While he poured the coffee, he made apparent social chit-chat. Where had they met each other? Where had they married, had they any brothers or sisters, parents who of course wanted to be grandparents, and what sort of work did Mr Quinn do? Though most of that information was already in the folder.

Mr Quinn was a surveyor like his father, and his father before him.

'Ah,' Dr Roxburgh smiled, 'you suffer as I do! A family tradition to live up to. My father was a doctor. So is my brother. What about you, Mrs Quinn?'

'One sister. One very fertile sister, with five children and another on the way.' Mrs Quinn pulled down the corners of her mouth in wistful envy.

'Life isn't fair, is it?' Dr Roxburgh commiserated. 'So we must see what can be done about it. Get you pregnant, if we can.' He paused. 'Now you'd like me to explain just what's involved in IVF?'

'If you would.'

'From the beginning?'

'Yes, please.'

'Now you know the chances are no more than one in three?'

The Quinns nodded.

'And that it will be a time of stress and strain, of

accepting, of disappointments and frustrations that will try the resolve and the patience of you both?'

'Yes.'

'Well, then,' Dr Roxburgh drew in a deep breath, 'to begin at the beginning. Let's look at a normal pregnancy.' He glanced from one intent face to the other. Neither of the Quinns looked embarrassed, only eager and curious. 'Midway in a normal conceptual cycle, there's a surge of luteinising hormone and ovulation occurs. The oocyte, that's the female egg, enters the fallopian tube. Got that?'

The Quinns nodded.

'Now we assume that sexual intercourse takes place, and, following that, sperm are deposited in the vagina. These travel up via the cervical canal and the uterus till they meet the egg in the fallopian tube. Fertilisation occurs, and the embryo undergoes a series of cell divisions as it makes its way down the fallopian tube, where it reaches the uterine cavity five days to a week later.'

'That,' Mrs Quinn murmured sadly, 'is in an ideal world. Not in mine.'

'Yes, you're right', agreed the doctor. 'What we have to find out is why the ideal isn't happening for you. And to try to help the ideal situation along.'

'We'll need more tests, I suppose?' Mr Quinn asked resignedly.

'Yes. It would seem that your cervix, Mrs Quinn, might be producing mucus hostile to the sperm. So I'd want to investigate that further. This coupled with Mr Quinn's low sperm mobility might well be preventing conception. We shall see.'

The doctor smiled encouragingly, and they both smiled with him. Despite the storminess of her feeling towards Dr Roxburgh, Lucy could not but admire his skill, possibly his *manipulative* skill, with people. Frequently husbands reacted strongly against any suggestion that the infertility might be partly due to them. Some months previously poor Mark Duffey had been punched in the jaw by a champion weight-lifter husband, when he was told he had a low sperm count and that his slender little wife had no other reason for not conceiving. It was doubtful, Lucy thought, that any husband, however tough, and however much he might feel his manhood was insulted, would ever attack Dr Roxburgh.

'So what can you do about it?' Mr Quinn asked urgently.

'Presuming that after all the tests we decide to take you on, you would begin a rigid timetable, either as out-patient or in-patient, starting at day one of your period, Mrs Quinn.'

'I'd stick to any timetable,' Mrs Quinn said. '*Anything.*'

'Then at the appropriate time in your cycle, when it seems ovulation is taking place, we would help everything along with an injection and recover the oocyte, keep it under sterile conditions, and after a while add a dilute solution of Mr Quinn's sperm. One of these will fertilise the oocyte. Is that clear so far?'

'Very clear.'

'Think of it as the creative process taking place outside the body,' advised Dr Roxburgh.

'How do you recover the oocyte. . .is it an operation?' asked Mrs Quinn.

'I insert a hollow needle. Nothing to it.'

'Then?'

'Then after about forty-eight hours the cell will have divided until there are about eight. Opinion varies as to when is the optimum time to transfer—whether at four, eight, or sixteen-cell stage. I favour the eight stage. You will then have another injection during the morning. And thirty-six hours later, the embryo will be returned to your body.'

'And is that the end?'

'Let's hope, Mrs Quinn, it's the beginning. Your body takes over, to accept and nurture your embryo. You should rest for a day afterwards, and we ask that you have no sexual intercourse until we know if you're pregnant or not.'

'How soon will we know?' she asked.

'You'll have a blood-test on the twelfth day. And if your period doesn't occur, you'll have an ultra-scan on the sixteenth.'

'Can I be with her, Doctor?' Mr Quinn asked.

'I positively insist that you are,' said Dr Roxburgh. 'It's a time when you need each other.' His expression momentarily softened. Perhaps his own need for Iris had come suddenly into his mind, thought Lucy. A need which maybe had driven him to those passionate kisses in the garden, and which they must both now forget.

For a moment the Quinns engaged him in questions about twins and triplets. Then finally he said briskly, 'Now I'm going to leave you with Sister. She's very knowledgeable, and I know she'll be helpful.' He glanced briefly in Lucy's direction. As she might have expected, his expression was no longer tender. His eyes were hostile, as if it were she who had behaved intolerably, not himself. A bitter question of his own seemed to hover on his lips. 'I expect there are questions you would like to ask her.'

The questions the Quinns wanted to ask her seemed endless.

They also wanted a peep at the unit itself, the clinical investigation room and Palmer Ward. It was seven twenty-five when they left.

Lucy took the lift up to the top floor, found Charles's apartment and rang the bell.

'Good heavens, Lucy, I thought you were never coming!' he greeted her. 'I thought you might have taken umbrage. . .been annoyed.'

'What about?'

'My telephone call.'

'Oh, that!' The strange thing was that Lucy had almost forgotten about it. Her mind was still on the Quinns, her grudging admiration for Dr Roxburgh's handling of them, and her puzzled resentment at his hostility to her. 'Why should I be annoyed?'

'It was from a woman,' Charles explained.

'We all gathered that,' Lucy said drily.

She flopped gratefully into the chair Charles waved her to. She was surprised at how tired she felt—tired and troubled. Even the magnificent view over the town with a fiery sunset behind it failed to rouse her normal enthusiasm.

'It might be only "Oh, that" to you, Lucy, but didn't you get my note?' Charles was busy at a drinks cabinet.

'Yes, I did—of course I did! Sorry, I'm still thinking of some new patients.'

'Well, enough's enough! Close the operating-theatre doors! What are you drinking? You've got to have at least one.'

Mindful of his last mixing of drinks, Lucy asked for a glass of wine or a sherry, or whatever he had opened.

'You said you'd had a shock,' she prompted as he handed her a glass of sherry.

'A ten-thousand volter.' He mopped his brow theatrically.

'Want to tell me?'

'If you've a mind to listen.' He pulled a chair up close to her. 'Do you remember that visit we did to Mrs Bowles?'

'Of course.'

'And how we got to know each other much better afterwards?'

'Yes,' said Lucy.

'And become really fond of each other?'

'Yes.'

Charles leaned forward and picked up her hand and held it between both of his, pressing it emotionally. For one wild moment she thought he was going to propose to her, and she tried to concentrate her mind on what on earth she would say.

'Remember we both found we'd been in love with someone else? A long time ago?'

'But that we weren't in love any longer,' Lucy put in, more for herself than for Charles.

Charles looked at her abstractedly, but neither agreed nor disagreed. Then he said, 'It was all a very long time ago as far as I was concerned. Nine years. And I'd never seen her since.' He sighed. 'Not once.'

Lucy cautiously sipped her drink and waited. 'What I didn't tell you was she was only seventeen,' he added. 'And she was pregnant.'

'How old were you?'

'Twenty-three—old enough to know better. I was still studying. But I wanted to marry her.'

'Did she want to marry you?'

'Oh, yes.'

'Why couldn't you?' she asked.

'Her parents wouldn't hear of it. They were rich and influential, and I wasn't good enough. They had their ambitions for her. They decided she must have an abortion. They took her off to South Africa.'

'Did you try to contact her?'

'Of course. I wrote to her old address, but my letters were returned.'

'And her name was Tamsin,' Lucy said slowly. 'That was the telephone call.'

'Yes.'

'Why? Why did she phone now?'

'She saw me on TV. Saw where I worked. Suddenly,' Charles spread his hands, 'we were back to the beginning again.'

'And the parents?' she queried.

'They divorced and remarried. They've lost interest in Tamsin. They've both got new families, new homes, new interests.'

'Oh. And Tamsin herself?'

'Living in Scotland.'

'Alone?' Lucy asked.

'No.'

'Married?'

'No.' Charles's voice shook. 'She has a daughter.'

'Your daughter?'

'Yes.'

'So she didn't have an abortion?'

'No.'

'That's wonderful!' Lucy exclaimed.

'Yes—in a way,' Charles admitted.

'What way isn't it?'

'I don't know, Lucy, I really don't know. I suppose this is all in me. This is a time when the counseller needs counselling.' He squeezed her fingers. 'What shall I do? After all these years, is it ever possible to go back? What do you think? And if it is, do I want to? Will Tamsin really want to?'

Lucy swallowed the rest of her glassful of sherry

at a single gulp and without demur allowed Charles to pour a refill. This was a time when Charles took a leaf out of his own counselling book and talked, when Charles the listener needed to be listened to. And who better to do it than herself? He talked of times he and Tamsin had had together, mixed with times with Lucy. It was as though he didn't know which was which and who he loved.

'What you love at twenty-three is so different from what you love in your thirties, Lucy,' he said. 'I want to see Tamsin—I want to see my daughter. I want to relate to them. And yet part of me wants to run a mile.'

After the second glass of sherry, he brought out some dry biscuits and a dish of olives, but he was too absorbed even to switch on the lamps. Darkness had fallen and the city lights were blossoming outside. Over the roofs came the ten sonorous chimes from the university clock.

'Don't worry,' said Charles as Lucy gave a start of surprise. 'I'll drive you home. We can buy a take-away and have it at your place.'

He resumed talking again about Tamsin, her youth, her charm, her loveliness. But now she might have changed, would certainly have changed, as he had done.

At this point, he grasped Lucy's hand and held it tightly. 'I've met you, and I'm very attracted to you. I'd begun to think I loved you.'

Lucy said soberly, 'Thinking isn't enough.'

'No, I don't mean that,' said Charles. 'I did love you—I do love you. but I'm not sure. . .'

It was past eleven when a knock sounded on the door.

'Oh, damn!' grumbled Charles. 'Who is it?' he called out loudly. 'Go away, I'm busy.'

The knock sounded again, more peremptorily this time.

'Look, it's time I went anyway,' said Lucy, getting to her feet, as Charles walked over and reluctantly opened the door.

An angry Dr Roxburgh stood at the other side, peering into the darkened sitting-room, his expression accusing.

'I was just about to drive Lucy home,' Charles explained, unusually ingratiating.

'I should damn well think so!'

'Did you want me for something, Rupert?'

'It can wait till morning,' said Dr Roxburgh, and turned on his heel.

There was a lamp burning in the lounge of Three, Laburnum Villas when Charles drove Lucy home, but the rest of the house was in darkness.

'Thanks, Lucy,' Charles cupped her face in his hands and kissed her lightly on the lips, 'you've been very sweet.'

She didn't invite him in, and he didn't seem to expect such an invitation.

'I'm sure things will work out,' she said, and waved him off.

When she opened the front door, she heard the sound of softly played music. In the lounge, Sergeant Sumner and Fenella had been sitting side by side on the sofa. They seemed to spring apart as guiltily and shyly as a pair of young teenagers.

Lucy smiled. 'Hi.' She hoped her expression was not forbidding, as Dr Roxburgh's had been just a short time ago.

'Hi,' they chorused.

'Would you like some coffee?' asked Fenella. 'I was just going to make some fresh. Meg's round at Andrew's.'

'Lovely! Then I'm off to bed. It's been one of those days.'

The next day was one of those too. Dr Roxburgh was showing a group of academic medics from the university round the unit, followed by a full clinic for laparoscopies and hysteroscopies. There was a problem with the Van der Pas hysteroscope, and it took Andrew's friend Mick an hour to fix it.

Mrs Parsons had a queue waiting for counselling and there was no sign of Charles. He had, it transpired, taken a week's leave for family reasons. And, to compound the day, Mr Armitage rang up to ask for urgent counselling for his wife.

Their session with Dr Roxburgh and Lucy lasted two gruelling hours.

'The trouble is,' Lucy told Meg that evening, 'I feel so sorry for them.'

'What about Dr Roxburgh?' asked Meg.

'He was obviously very concerned.'

'But he feels there's nothing more he can do?'

'They could try GIFT,' said Lucy.

'Gamete intra-fallopian transfer?'

'Yes. But he thought the chances were zero. And he thinks Mrs Armitage has been through enough.'

'What does *she* think?' Meg stirred some scrambled eggs. They were both too tired to cook anything more complicated.

'She seems to feel she's had enough.'

'What do you think?'

'I'd be reluctant to see her embark on another programme. She's exhausted. You can't go on stimulating the ovaries, taking hormones, going through tests and scans and proddings and pokings indefinitely.'

'Sad!' sighed Meg.

'I'll tell you, the counselling was sad,' Lucy agreed. 'They're such good people.'

'So what did you tell them? Butter that toast while you're telling me, will you, love?'

'The usual. Dr Roxburgh suggested adoption. But they'd been down that road.'

'Rejected?' queried Meg.

'Yes, over and over again. Mr Armitage's age,' Lucy explained.

'I don't think age matters. There are some very good older fathers, and some rotten young ones.'

'They have their rules.'

'I suppose so.' Meg spooned the fluffy egg on to the toast.

'Eat that while it's hot and I'll tell you something

else.' She waited till Lucy had picked up her knife and fork, then she said, 'I've seen quite a bit of the Armitages, and I don't know if it's a good or a bad thing. They're often up in the nursery. No, it wasn't counting chickens. They came up to see Little Boy Blue. They've bought him all sorts of things. And nearly every day they come in to give him a cuddle. They reckon a baby needs cuddling, and they're right. We nurses don't have enough time. But they do.'

'Do you think they want to adopt him?' asked Lucy.

'They'd give their eye teeth to.'

'Even though he may not be well?'

'Especially because he isn't well. They reckon he's going to need a lot of care, a lot of money spent on him.'

'Do you think there's any chance?' Lucy queried.

'No,' Meg shook her head vigorously. 'They've slightly more chance because he's sick. But he'll have to go through the proper adoption procedure, and I don't rate their chances very high—they've been turned down so often. Well, eat up, don't cry into my best scrambled egg! Let's talk about something cheerful! Andrew and I worked out a good idea for the fancy-dress Ball.'

'I thought you were going to be on duty?'

'So I am. It's for you and Fenella and Andrew. So you can keep an eye on him.'

'I don't like the sound of this,' Lucy pretended to grimace.

'You will when you hear what it is.'

'What?'

'Three little maids from school. You know—from *The Mikado*. All nice black shiny wigs and silk kimonos. It'll go down a bomb! Andrew's coming round later to discuss details, so look out anything you might be throwing away.'

For the rest of the evening, they tried to dismiss Little Boy Blue and the Armitages. The three of them sketched out their ideas for the costumes, looked through their clothes for any item that could be cut up, and the ravages of the day were almost but not quite forgotten.

Just before Andrew said goodnight, Meg asked Lucy, 'Any idea what Charles is going as?'

'I don't know if he's going at all. He's off on holiday.'

'Holiday? Just like that?'

'I think it's more leave for family reasons than just holiday.'

'Hey, just a moment!' exclaimed Meg. 'Was it anything to do with that mysterious phone call?'

'I think it might have been,' Lucy admitted.

'She sounded like a VIPP—a Very Important Person from his Past.'

'Yes.'

'You think he's off to meet her?'

Lucy said slowly, 'I hope so.'

Meg put her arm round Lucy's shoulder. 'You poor lass! Like you say, it's been one of those days!'

CHAPTER TEN

CHARLES didn't return by the day of the fancy-dress Ball.

He telephoned Lucy to say he had arranged to take a little longer. There was a chance he would be able to travel back on the Saturday, but could she get someone else to use his ticket just in case. She couldn't tell from his voice whether or not the reunion had gone well.

'Well, Andrew will keep an eye on you and vice versa,' Meg remarked philosophically when Lucy told her the news. As she pointed out, with her on duty, Andrew needed a partner. He was, of course, very much in the partnership, the life and soul of the three little maids.

For the week preceding the dance there had been much snipping of remnants and crêpe paper, much cutting up of old garments, as well as visits to the newly opened theatre shop in the town.

That Saturday evening, Lucy was alone at Number Three. Meg had left for the hospital. Fenella had been out for the afternoon with Sergeant Sumner and was going to get into her costume in the changing-room at Physio. Lucy dressed herself in her outfit—a long dark wig, with giant glittering combs and blue kimono, and waited, wondering if Charles would telephone, half hoping he would, half hoping he wouldn't.

At seven-thirty, Andrew rang the doorbell. He and his friends had clubbed together for a taxi, and it awaited Lucy outside.

Inside were bearded nursemaid and moustached baby. The pram was stowed in the boot.

Lucy stepped inside. They asked her advice on make-up, bemoaned the fact that they might well be outshone by a group of housemen who were going as a hairy corps de ballet, but tactfuly avoided asking about Charles—then, as the taxi swept up to the hospital entrance, reminded her to save a dance for each of them.

The dance was held in the conference-room of the main wing of the hospital, a large and impressive panelled room on the far side of the administrative offices and conveniently removed from most of the wards. It had been skilfully decorated by the friends of the Hartington with bunting and fresh flowers, and the band, which included members of staff, had already begun to play.

Music throbbed out to greet them. Multi-coloured lights spilled out through the long windows, and dancers threw dark mysterious shadows over the tarmac and the grass.

Lucy's first dance was with Andrew, till Mr Yates, the baker, stepped forward to separate them. 'Can't have two young ladies dancing together,' he laughed, 'while us poor men stand on the sidelines.'

His wife was at home with the prize-winning twins, but the Yates were great hospital supporters.

Because of the wide age range of the company, the band alternated modern music with 1950s and 60s hits, and the programme included waltzes and valetas, the Gay Gordons and a dash of Country and Western.

Despite Charles's absence, despite even Dr Roxburgh's forthcoming wedding, Lucy began to enjoy herself. The music was good, the costumes colourful and clever. It was fun trying to identify with whom one was dancing.

Waltzing with a gorilla, she found—only when heat drove him to remove his headpiece—that it was Mr Beamish, the world's leading expert on embryology. A long-eared Mr Spock was the registrar cardiologist, and a very large Little Red Riding Hood was none other than Sergeant Sumner, who had mistaken Little Maid Lucy and Little Maid Fenella.

But there was no disguising Rupert Roxburgh. Someone once said that a woman saw with her heart and not with her eyes, and Lucy's heart recognised with a quick and untidy leap the dishevelled pirate in the high sea-boots, with a black patch over his eye and a black woolly beard over most of the rest of his face.

He was right to come as a pirate, she thought.

Then it was like a caricatured repeat of their first meeting. Inexorably, he was coming across the room towards her.

Instinctively she drew away. She wouldn't dance

with him. She couldn't dance with him. She would rush out. She would make excuses. She would simply refuse.

She *was* dancing with him, her body melting into his, her feet following his, butterfly-light, her head close to his chest, fancying she heard the rhythm of his heart.

'I owe you a profound apology,' he said almost at once, tilting his head and shoulders back from her, so that his unpatched eye could look piercingly into her face. 'I behaved intolerably the last time we were alone together—inexcusably! It's been very much on my mind.'

Lucy shrugged. 'We were both very tense.'

He gave a short, almost angry bark of laughter. 'That isn't sufficient excuse. I don't make a habit of. . .' But he didn't say of what. Instead, he added, very soberly, 'I promise it won't happen again. Do you accept that?'

'Why, yes.' She looked up, surprised, not sure what was coming, not sure what she wanted to come.

The music had stopped and everyone was clapping, but neither Lucy nor Dr Roxburgh seemed aware of it. They stood facing each other, their hands at their sides, staring into each other's face as if trying to read the maps of some distant and dangerous territory.

'Do you trust me, Lucy?'

The question was unexpected. Now it was her turn to give a short derisive laugh. 'In some ways. Not in others.'

The band had started up again, and automatically he put his arms round her. Automatically she let herself be swept away.

'But you trust me when I say it won't happen again?'

'Oh, yes, I trust you in that.' She was surprised at the bitterness with which she snapped that back. But the bitterness seemed not to matter. In fact, it seemed to please him.

'Good!' He swirled her round expertly, then brought her close again and added, 'Because something has cropped up.'

For one wild elated wonderful moment, it occurred to Lucy that what had cropped up might be that Dr Iris wasn't coming over, that Dr Iris and he were not going to get married after all.

But such magic moments only happen in fairytales or soap operas.

'What's cropped up?' she asked, as, with a final roll of drums, the music stopped.

Lightly Dr Roxburgh put his hand under her elbow and began to escort her over to the table by the window where Andrew, Fenella and Sergeant Sumner were drinking strawberry fizzes. He stopped a few yards short of them. 'I've been invited back to the Royal East Anglia to give a lecture on IVF,' he told her.

'Congratulations,' she said in what she hoped was an appropriate tone of voice.

'I had a phone call this afternoon. There's a big international conference.'

'Splendid!'

'And they want me to take you along as well. You must be one of the most experienced IVF sisters in the country. The thinking being. . .'

Lucy hardly listened to the rest of it. She was filled with pain and panic. She opened her mouth to say she couldn't, wouldn't do it.

But then he went on, 'I wanted to make sure that you wouldn't,' he raised one visible eyebrow deprecatingly, 'find my company too distasteful.'

Lucy shook her head in silence. And, ever master of the moment, he walked her back to her friends, smiling urbanely as if nothing of any importance had happened.

Possibly to him, it hadn't.

'I'm delivering you back one little maid, still a virtuous little schoolgirl,' he told the others.

And then, with a bow, he disappeared into the multi-coloured crowd that had begun to gather round the white-draped tables, as a powerful hospital rumour gathered strength that the serving of cold supper had begun.

'This is where we remember poor Meg,' Andrew smiled. 'She said she didn't mind about the dancing, but she did mind about the buffet.'

'I'll go up first,' offered Lucy. 'Even if you are the third little maid, you'll still have to stand back from the buffet while we ladies are served.'

They all drifted over towards the tables, and Lucy picked up a tray and began loading it.

Meg had a penchant for vol-au-vents of all fla-vours, and there were all her favourites there—chicken, prawn, mushroom, crab. There were mountains of fresh-cut sandwiches and little pud-dings and sweets in handy cups and bowls for loading on trays.

'Surely you're not going to eat all that, Lucy?' Dr Driscoll, the cardiologist, asked her anxiously, and muttered about cholesterol as she threaded her way towards the staircase.

'No,' Lucy smiled and shook her head, 'these are to be shared among three.'

'Well, don't let them make a habit of it.' He shook the feathers of his Red Indian head-dress chidingly.

Outside the conference-room, the corridor, then the panelled hall were deserted. Visiting time was over. But a late visitor was just crossing the hall—a girl with spiky yellow hair. An elusive memory stirred and was gone. The night porter in the glassed-in reception office was doing the pools. He looked up and waved to Lucy as she passed.

Lucy stepped on to the escalator and glided upwards. Andrew's assistant was coming down on the other escalator, carrying the perennial tray of blood samples. Each lifted a free hand in greeting as the escalator sped them their different ways.

Inside Maternity, Meg was in the kitchen, check-ing bottles. She looked round at Lucy, her rosy face smiling.

'Having a good time?' she asked.

'Fabulous!' Lucy smiled back.

'Even without Charles?'

Lucy nodded and brought out the tray from behind her back. She put it down on the plastic worktop.

'You're a pal! Mind you, I'm not sure you should have left Andrew alone with all those lovely girls downstairs!'

'That's all right, he's safe enough,' Lucy smiled. 'Everyone thinks he's another lovely girl.'

'No kidding?'

'No kidding! Old Dr McGrath. . .'

'Him who was consultant here when babies were being potty-trained at six weeks old?'

'The same.'

'He's supposed to be ninety-five next month,' commented Meg.

'So he is. Well, he told Andrew he was as pretty a girl as he'd ever met at the hospital.'

'That doesn't say much for us, eh?' Meg pretended to bridle. 'Well,' she eyed the tray of goodies, 'I'll go and tell the nurses to come and help themselves. The mums are still awake. Do go and show them your costume—they'd like that.'

There was a particularly poor choice of television programme on that night, so the mothers greeted Lucy's appearance with enthusiasm. They examined the costume with great care, getting ideas, they said, for when their babies were dressing up for school plays.

'You wait till you see Andrew—Sister Meg's

fiancé—then you'll be quite bowled over,' Lucy told them.

'OK, you've earned your reward.' Meg came through into the ward, licking the last crumb off her lips. 'Five minutes in the nursery!'

She watched Lucy make straight for Little Boy Blue's cot. 'He gets sweeter every day,' she said, as they bent over it.

Then they both exclaimed together. Tucked precariously close to the fragile body was a small yellow teddy bear of the kind that moulted its fur at a touch. In fact, Boy Blue's tiny fist already held a strand of it.

With an indignant exclamation Meg snatched the offending toy away. 'Who could have been stupid enough to give him that?' she exclaimed.

Lucy shook her head.

'Not one of my nurses,' Meg said stoutly.

'Not the Armitages, surely?'

'No, certainly not!'

'Someone at visiting time?'

'Could be.'

'Who else comes in?'

'One of the cleaning ladies? They're all so sorry for him. Mrs Brown is always saying he isn't long for this world. He won't be, if they do that.' Meg clucked indignantly. 'When will people learn that misplaced kindness can kill?'

Returning to the dance-floor, Lucy had a decorous dance with Dr McGrath, who made no more startling comments other than that she had some very pretty friends. She watched the housemen's corps de ballet put on a lively display of high-kicking hairy legs. She glimpsed the pirate in the audience that roared its applause, but he didn't come near her again.

At home that night, she slept fitfully. When she did drift off, she dreamed of the yellow teddy and Little Boy Blue, all mixed up with a girl with spiky yellow hair, of misplaced kindness, of a bold bad pirate making her walk the plank, and somehow she knew if she did walk it, she would fall, not into the sea. . .

But into a hopeless, dangerous unreturned love.

CHAPTER ELEVEN

CHARLES returned from his leave of absence in an unreadable mood.

At the Tuesday case conference Lucy saw Dr Roxburgh eyeing him thoughtfully, his gaze flicking occasionally from Charles's to Lucy's face.

Charles had briefly popped his head round her door a few minutes before the meeting, 'Just to touch base, Lucy! Had an interesting leave; tell you about it later.'

Lucy tried to concentrate on the meeting. The discussion centred on the possibility of expanding their GIFT treatment, then went on about the three new patients, awaiting IVF. In Charles's absence, Mrs Parsons had counselled them, and Dr Roxburgh had appointments with them for next Wednesday.

'After that,' he announced pleasantly, 'I shall be away for all of Thursday, Mark as usual standing in. I'll be at the Royal East Anglia's IVF conference. So will Sister.' He nodded in Lucy's direction.

'Shall you be giving a talk, Lucy?' asked Mark.

'Oh, she'll say a few words, won't you, Sister?' Dr Roxburgh said breezily, and, without giving her time to agree or deny, he went on. 'However, Mark,' he smiled, 'we shall certainly be back in good time for your farewell party.'

Mark smiled back totally without malice and reminded him, 'And Dr Morton's welcome party.'

If he was being got rid of by Dr Roxburgh, dear stick-in-the-mud Dr Duffey appeared to have no idea of it.

Everybody laughed as though the reminder had very special significance. Everyone, that was, except Lucy.

'You're right, Mark.' Dr Roxburgh smiled with such tender pleasure that Lucy felt guilty at begruding him his happiness, 'I can't let that slip my mind. That's one party I can't miss!'

And everyone laughed approvingly again.

Charles interrupted his laughter to raise his brows several times meaningly in Lucy's direction, as if to signal, What did I tell you? But she elected not to see.

It was nearly twelve-thirty when Dr Roxburgh finally collected his reports and files and papers together and stood up.

Charles hung back as everyone else filed out. He stood leaning against the radiator, his arms folded across his chest, like a man who didn't quite know how to say what he had to say.

'So you enjoyed your time off?' Lucy asked gently.

He drew a deep breath, unfolded his arms, and spread his hands. 'Oh, yes, Lucy, I think I did.'

'Do you want to talk about it?' she prompted gently again.

Charles thrust out his lower lip. He appeared to hesitate. 'Not really. I'm not sure—at least, not yet.'

Lucy nodded, but said nothing.

'I'm in a state of what we psychiatrists call cognitive dissonance,' he added.

Lucy smiled. 'What my mother would call swithering. Not being able to make up your mind.'

'I can and I can't.'

'Same thing,' she told him.

'I mean. . . I don't know. . .and Tamsin doesn't know.'

'Did you meet your daughter?' Lucy asked.

'Oh, yes!'

'That must have been wonderful!'

'I have a photo of her.' Charles opened his wallet and displayed the photograph of a pretty chubby-faced little lass in pigtails.

'She's lovely! She's got your eyes.'

'Do you think so?' And then, 'I must say you've been very understanding about all this. I mean, you might have thought. . .in fact, at one time, I thought. . .'

Lucy glanced up at the clock on the wall, thankful that she had to be in the clinic in five minutes' time.

Charles took the hint and stood up. 'At least let me buy you lunch. Canteen at what time?'

'Sorry!' Lucy shook her head. 'We've got a full schedule, and I'm working through. I'll be grabbing a sandwich as and when.'

He was behaving just like Dr Roxburgh all those years ago, she thought wryly, buying her a meal over which to take his leave. Only it was different this time. This time, she didn't mind.

'OK, you workaholic, some other time,' Charles smiled cheerfully. Opening the door, he paused. 'What's all this about you and the big chief swanning off to Cambridge?'

'Duty! He's giving a talk. And it appears I'm giving one too.'

Charles laughed derisively. 'Well, mind Dr Iris doesn't have anything to complain about!'

Lucy didn't deign to answer.

For the rest of that day Charles kept a low and almost invisible profile. 'Catching up on my backlog of work,' he told Lucy as he swept past her two days later in the corridor. 'Pile of reports this high!' He indicated the ceiling and then dived smartly into his office.

But on the Wednesday afternoon he managed to pop his head round her door and say, 'Sock it to them, Lucy! Tell them at the Royal East Anglian how good we are here!' Then he was off again.

'You must be tickled pink,' Meg said later that evening. 'Going back to your old hospital and telling them a thing or two.'

'Oh, I don't suppose I'll be telling them anything they don't know,' answered Lucy. 'And I'm not tickled pink. I'm terrified!'

And, she added to herself, for more reasons than just giving a lecture.

'Experience in this field is invaluable,' Meg replied sententiously. 'And everyone's experience is just that bit different. We do things differently here from, say, Boston or Cambridge or Miami or the Henrico. And in IVF we're beginning to lead. Under Dr Roxburgh, we'll lengthen that lead.'

'You reckon?'

'I do more than reckon.' Meg began to tidy away before they went to bed. 'I *know*.'

Lucy smiled indulgently. 'Three cheers for the Dr Roxburgh fan club!'

'You may smile, young Lucy! But there *is* such a thing!'

Passing behind Lucy's chair, Meg ruffled her hair affectionately. Soberly and gently she added, 'I wish it had turned out differently.'

'What do you mean?' queried Lucy.

But Meg just shook her head and wouldn't explain. 'Want to borrow anything of mine for tomorrow? My new tan handbag? Those clip earrings you lust after? They'd go well with your linen suit and the peach blouse.'

Lucy laughed. 'Thanks, but I've got some little pearl ones, remember? I wouldn't mind borrowing a bit of your aplomb, though!'

They both smiled.

'Do you reckon there'll be anyone left from your day?' Meg asked.

Lucy shrugged. 'Possibly. But the ones I knew best all seem to have scattered.'

'That's nursing for you.' Meg walked over to her bedroom. 'Well, I'm off to bed. See you in the morning!'

The morning was cool and bright, a typical September morn with a soft pink and blue sky and a breath of mist. Lucy, garbed in her smart linen suit and apricot blouse, waited, with mixed feelings, mostly of trepidation, for the sound of Dr Roxburgh's car.

'Good luck with the lecture!' Meg threw over her shoulder as she and Fenella closed the front door behind them.

'You'll be fine,' Fenella shouted reassuringly as they set off for work. Lucy listened to their footsteps going down the path to the pavement, then the house fell silent.

Punctually at eight, Lucy heard a car come to a halt outside Number Three. She was at the door before Dr Roxburgh had time to ring the bell.

'"Punctuality is the politeness of princes,"' he quoted approvingly. 'And of princesses, I see!' adding in the same breath, 'You look very. . .' he stopped himself before the last word and turned it into a non-word, or at least a non-compliment '. . .nice!'

'Thank you,' said Lucy as he held the car door open for her.

'Very nice indeed!'

She thanked him again.

'Nervous?' he asked as he started the engine and eased the car away from the kerb.

'A little.'

'Of the lecture or me?'

'Both.'

He laughed.

'There's really no need—on both counts. The audience will love you. And I. . .' he took his hand off the wheel in a gesture of finality '. . .well, you know my situation.'

'Yes.'

'So. . .' he guided the Rover out of the mêlée of town traffic, '. . .let's talk about something else. Or would you rather not talk at all? Would you rather look at your lecture notes? And I'll concentrate,' he smiled sideways at her, 'on getting you there safely.'

'Yes, I'd like to learn my notes,' Lucy accepted gratefully. Though she knew her notes off by heart, their study was a refuge. And it was a choice that seemed to please Dr Roxburgh.

'Would you like some music?' he asked as silent mile after silent mile sped by. The town scenery changed to twiggy hedgerows and woods, then smooth up-and-down hills between fields of sheep-cropped grass.

'If you would.'

He shrugged, and raised his brows wryly at her studiedly neutral responses. We're like shadow-boxers, she thought miserably, aware of each other, oh, so painfully aware, but unable to reach out and touch. Why? Because he was in love with Dr Iris Morton, and neither dared allow their previous feelings to overwhelm them.

'You liked Chopin, as I recall,' he said.

'I still do.' For some reason, tears sprang to her eyes.

'You haven't changed in that, at least.'

She looked at him sideways. She wanted to ask him if he thought she had changed in other ways, but she couldn't find the words.

'It doesn't bring back painful memories?' he asked.

'Memories. But not painful ones.'

'Good!'

Lucy closed her eyes as the Chopin prelude softly filled the car, and the memories that flooded in were almost unbearably painful, sharp with thoughts of what might have been. Rupert had taken her to a concert at a country house near Cambridge. They had walked along the terrace to the sound of the prelude.

'Can you remember when?' he asked her suddenly.

She kept her eyes closed because otherwise the tears would have escaped and answered, 'The centenary concert.'

On the excuse of looking out at the undulating countryside, she turned her head and stealthily wiped her eyes.

'You were wearing a dress that same colour.' He took a hand off the wheel and touched the cuff of her apricot blouse. 'And you wore a bow in the nape of your neck. And in the concert you kicked off your shoes and you lost one.'

'They were new,' she protested.

'I gathered that. Too new and too high!'

'I'm surprised you remembered.'

'Oh, I remember,' he said, and, lest she thought he remembered for anything connected to her, he added, 'My life took on a change shortly after that.'

Of course, she thought. It was almost immediately after that that the young researcher Dr Iris arrived and the rumours began.

Now the Rover began racing through the beginnings of the Fens, and soon above the tops of the willows could be seen the towers and spires of Cambridge.

Once in the suburbs, cars and lorries slowed them up. Finally they came to a full stop in a traffic jam opposite Romano's plushy restaurant.

Rupert jerked his thumb towards the Georgian façade and the crested swinging sign. 'I invited a girl to dinner there once,' he said, almost musingly. 'But she stood me up.'

The remark was so unexpected that for a moment Lucy was lost for words. Then as steadily and clearly as she could, she said, 'That was because she knew only too well what she was going to hear.'

He said no more. It was as though she hadn't spoken. Five minutes later they were driving between the tall pillars of the Royal East Anglia Hospital, and Rupert Roxburgh was pointing to the great dark five-storey façade.

'Well,' he commented, 'they don't seem to have done much to the old place since our day.'

Lucy agreed that it looked exactly the same. Too much the same, she thought, with too many memories.

'Now comes the most difficult part of the trip. Finding a place to park!'

Rupert swung the car in and out of the twistings of the perimeter lane, looking in vain for a vacant place.

Then he stopped at the back entrance. 'Not so far for you to walk.' He opened the car door. 'There we are!' he said with a certain gritty brightness. 'One sister delivered safe and sound. And not too much of an ordeal, I hope. See you on the platform, if I don't see you before. I expect you'll find there's a welcome committee inside.'

There was indeed, and a partly familiar one. Almost immediately as Lucy entered the old Victorian marble hall, Nesta, dressed now in a senior sister's uniform, came rushing over to greet her.

'Lovely to see you again!' she cooed, brushing Lucy's cheek with her powdered one. 'But where's the man of the moment, Dr Roxburgh?' She giggled. 'You haven't left him behind, surely?'

'He's just parking the car,' Lucy told her.

'Well, let me look at you! You look fine! A little thinner. Married yet?'

Lucy shook her head.

'On the brink?'

'Not really.'

'Oh, bad luck! Living with anyone? A man, I mean?'

'No.'

Nesta showed her left hand proudly. 'I'm married,

for my sins. Well, it happens to the best of us,
doesn't it? Even my baby brother's married. You
know. . . Peter, the one who bet me I couldn't make
you stand up Rupert Roxburgh and come to his
graduation party instead.'

'I didn't know he had,' said Lucy.

'Had what, dear? Married or made you stand up
Rupert?'

'Stand up,' Lucy replied in a strangled voice.

'Oh, that was nothing! Just a bit of harmless
medical student nonsense! And anyway, Rupert *did*
go off with that woman doctor, didn't he? Probably
married to her now.'

'Not quite.'

Fortunately at that point a tall, bald-headed man
came up and introduced himself as the Royal East
Anglia's IVF consultant. He had a younger man in
tow and a group of newly qualified doctors embark-
ing on postgraduate research. Behind her, Lucy was
aware that Rupert Roxburgh had appeared, and was
joining in the chat.

'I've found out you're speaking at twelve-thirty,'
he came and whispered in her ear. 'That's a good
time. And after that you can relax and enjoy a good
hospital lunch.'

He laughed wryly. He seemed easier with her now
that he was in company, their roles defined, a kindly
consultant with his hardworking sister.

'When are you speaking?' she asked him.

'After lunch.' He turned his eyes up to the ceiling.
'The post-prandial hour when everyone falls asleep.

He looked about him. 'We seem to be moving.' He put his hand under her elbow to guide her towards the lecture hall. 'Now remember, you've nothing to be nervous about. They're all eager to learn. If there are any questions you can't answer, tell them to ask again at my lecture.'

The hall was even bigger than Lucy remembered it, perhaps because she had never been on the dais before, and it was much more densely packed.

It seemed to Lucy that Dr Roxburgh kept his eyes on her face from the moment she rose to her feet to the moment she sat down, amid healthily loud applause. For some reason she found his gaze neither disconcerting nor distracting. Just twice in her question time she glanced in his direction and pondered whether or not she should refer the question to him.

But she didn't. She struggled through.

Lunch was quite a luxurious affair of roast chicken and lots of bought-in creamy puddings, with vases of thornless roses on the top table.

Nesta was also sitting there. Just before the puddings were served, she leaned across and asked Lucy if she didn't find it difficult to empathise with a married woman's need for motherhood, her being single and never having, as it were. . .?

But it was Dr Roxburgh, sitting on the other side of the consultant seminologist, who answered. 'Do you find it difficult to empathise with a patient who's fractured his skull. . .you never, as it were,' gently he mimicked her words, 'having fractured yours? Or someone wanting a sex change. . .you, I'm sure never, having wanted that?'

'No fear!' exclaimed Nesta, and, suitably chastened, said no more for the rest of the meal. But all sorts of thoughts were going round Lucy's mind. Now that she could relax after the disciplined concentration on what she was going to say in her lecture, the full impact of what Nesta had told her in the hall could be examined.

As the doctors talked medical shop, she was thinking, so. . .it had all been 'harmless medical student nonsense'. Weren't those the words Nesta had used? Had she too easily believed in a pack of untruths? The little jump her heart gave at that thought was calmed by commonsense reasoning. Nesta and her brother had not misled her about Dr Iris. Dr Roxburgh had gone with her to America, and now she was going to follow him back. And now they were to be married.

No one seemed to notice Lucy's absorbed silence. For everyone else, lunch passed off smoothly.

Then it was Dr Roxburgh's lecture. It was unequivocally the success of the conference. He was a natural speaker—he had a rich, pleasing voice, a relaxed manner, a natural delivery and an innate delicacy and sympathy for a subject so hedged round with emotion and inhibition. All this leavened with just the right amount of humour.

Post-prandial hour it might be, but no one fell asleep. This time applause was not enough. Spontaneously, everyone in the audience got to their feet.

Teatime was a lengthy business because people wanted to go on asking questions. But a pale autumn sun was still shining by the time Dr Roxburgh accelerated the Rover out of the hospital gates and headed south. 'What did I tell you?' Rupert said lightly as they left the environs of Cambridge behind. 'You were first-class! I was proud of you.'

She gave a little laugh. 'But you were right at the top of the first division.'

'Oh, I'm an old hand!'

They exchanged quick glances—tremulous, momentarily loving.

'Lucy,' Rupert said gravely, as the traffic thinned, the countryside widened, 'can I talk to you like an old friend?'

She shrugged. She wanted to shout out that she didn't want to be an old friend, an old flame, an old anything. Besides, she'd had experience of his talks as an old friend.

'We got to know each other better again today, didn't we? I realise. . .' He hesitated while he negotiated round a large petrol tanker, 'I realise what you're going through. I know what it's like to love someone, and that someone to love someone else.'

Words failed her. She nodded, and kept her eyes on her folded hands.

'It's hell. But it will pass, I promise you.'

Lucy bit her lips to stop them trembling. She was aware that he had glanced sideways to see how she was taking all this. She turned her head to look through the window and avoid his scrutiny.

The road was spinning them like a grey spool through the greeny-brown rounded hills. Her day had been like that—up and down. Moments of fear and tension, moments of triumph and pleasure and a beguiling empathy.

Glimpses of happiness that might have been. Now down into the hollow. Now here he was telling her she would soon get over him. Humiliation scorched her cheeks. There would be no greater humiliation than that. She had been a fool to allow herself to nurture such a hopeless love for all these years.

Apparently aware of her distress, Rupert Roxburgh kept his eyes fixed on the rising road ahead.

As if from a long way away, she noticed a caravan lumbering downhill in the opposite direction.

Then suddenly, just before they drew level, a red car pulled out from behind the caravan, accelerating impatiently to overtake.

Lucy remembered letting out a cry of horror, as Rupert stood on the brake and twisted the steering-wheel to avoid a head-on collision.

There was a bang as the front tyre burst, the smell of burned rubber and scorched brakes. The Rover skidded halfway into the ditch. Lucy put out her hand and felt a sharp pain.

Everything happened in a mixture of slow and accelerated motion. She was aware that the red car had wobbled, its tyres screaming—but by a whisker had managed to get back in behind the caravan.

It came to an abrupt halt, and a shamefaced driver

emerged. 'Sorry, sir! Sorry!' he kept saying over and over again. 'You were hidden in the dip. Honestly, I thought the road was clear. Then the next minute. . .' He mopped his brow. 'You did a wonderful job, sir, avoiding us! I'm very grateful. Is your wife hurt, sir? Oh, help, there's blood on her hand!'

Lucy could remember looking down, apparently dispassionately, at the blood on her hand, and then, good nurse though she was, she fainted.

Within seconds she came to with Dr Roxburgh carrying her in his arms across the road, and at the same time delivering a Roxburgh lecture on not-overtaking-till-you're-certain-the-road-is-clear to the driver of the red car. The man was still murmuring incoherent apologies.

The driver of the caravan produced a chair, which with an imperious, 'I'm a doctor,' Rupert Roxburgh placed her in, and set about, as he called it, 'running the ruler over her.'

'There's a first-aid box in my car,' he told the red-car driver. 'Get it, please! Now, my darling,' he said softly, 'let's have a good look at you!'

At least that was what Lucy thought he said, but she must have misheard. Misinterpreted, too, the tender look in his eyes behind the careful clinical expertise with which he examined her.

'Pulse a little fluttery.' He shook his head chidingly, releasing her wrist.

'Can you wonder?' she croaked, for many reasons.

'I suppose not. Now,' without taking his eyes off

her face, he took the first-aid box the red-car driver held out to him, 'let's look at that hand! Mmm, it's none too deep,' he said, carefully swabbing away the blood. 'You can flex your fingers all right? Good!' He smiled at her as he applied the dressing. 'This isn't really my field. You'd probably do it a whole lot better.'

Yet such was the anaesthetising effect of shock that, as she watched his thin skilful fingers at work on her hand, she thought she had never felt happier in her life.

Then a police car came racing up, its siren screaming, its blue light twinkling, followed by an ambulance and a breakdown truck.

Darkness had fallen before the Rover was pulled clear. 'Take us till morning to get her on the road again,' the mechanic told Dr Roxburgh.

Rupert Roxburgh swore softly.

'There's a motel of sorts in the village. Nothing special, of course,' the mechanic suggested. 'We'll have the car ready for you at eight-thirty.'

'I'd be obliged if you would,' Dr Roxburgh said shortly. 'It's important I'm back by noon.'

At last he turned to Lucy again. 'Sorry about this.'

'All my fault,' said the driver of the red car lugubriously. 'At least let me give you and your wife a lift to the motel.'

For some reason, Rupert Roxburgh chose not to contradict the man. But at the rather seedy little motel he made the position crystal clear.

'Two single rooms for my colleague and myself,' he ordered crisply.

'If you say so, sir.' The stout lady behind the reception counter looked disbelieving. She hooked the keys off the wall and plonked them down on the counter.

'There, sir!' she said. 'Two single rooms.' She winked at Lucy. 'Side by side.'

'Goodnight, Lucy. Sleep as well as you can,' said Rupert. Then he added something about someone being a fool. The red-car driver, probably, but it sounded like Charles.

For the rest of that disturbed night, Lucy tossed and turned. On the other side of what seemed no thicker than a cardboard partition wall, she could hear Rupert Roxburgh tossing and turning too.

Towards dawn she must have fallen asleep, for she dreamed that the door had opened and Rupert had come in.

She opened her eyes. She wasn't dreaming. Dr Roxburgh was standing in the doorway of her room, fully dressed, thrusting out his left hand and pointing at his wrist watch.

'Come on, Lucy, it's after nine! You've just time to grab some coffee. . .and we'll be on our way!'

He was a totally different person from the tender concerned man of the previous evening. His mind seemed entirely set on getting safely back to the Hartington well before noon.

Two and a half hours later, she found out why.

As they neared the hospital grounds, he asked

her, 'Shall I drop you at the hospital or at home, Lucy?'

'The hospital will be fine. I'm not on duty, but I'd like to have a word with Mrs Parsons.'

He nodded abstractedly, as if he had lost all interest in her and her arrangements. Then suddenly, as they pulled round to the main entrance, he stiffened. His whole attention was focused on an airport taxi just drawing up.

Out of it stepped a slender woman with close-cropped dark hair.

In a moment, Rupert Roxburgh had stopped the Rover immediately behind the taxi and was bounding across the intervening space.

Iris!' he shouted. 'Iris! You're early!'

The girl turned. Her thin face lit up.

'Rupert! Rupert, darling!' she cried, and flew into his arms.

CHAPTER TWELVE

Two days later, Charles put a friendly arm round Lucy's shoulder and murmured, 'I've something to tell you!'

They had just counselled two couples seeking IVF treatment, and Lucy was sitting at her desk, writing up her notes. She turned and raised her brows invitingly.

'I'm considering moving out of my flat. I'm considering capitulating.'

'To Dr Iris's charms?' she queried.

'Not exactly. I had a little note from the administrator to say he'd like to be able to offer it to Dr and Mrs Roxburgh. You can read it if you want to.' He tried to hand her a letter, but she waved it away.

'Oh!' she said noncommittally.

'And—shall we say?—it might be mutually convenient. . .mutually convenient to them and us. You see, Tamsin. . .' he hesitated '. . . Tamsin wants to buy a house of. . .our own. A flat isn't really suitable for a family. And,' he looked like a man who was bursting with happiness, but who reckoned he ought to try for the sake of his hearer to conceal it, 'we are a family. We're three.'

'Are you telling me that you and Tamsin are to be married?' asked Lucy.

'Yes.'

'Wonderful!' She went over and put her arms round him. 'I'm delighted!'

'I thought you ought to be the first to know. We're not telling anyone else yet.' Charles bent down and kissed her. 'You've been very understanding.'

Rupert Roxburgh, putting his head round the door at that moment, frowned and withdrew.

'Take no notice, Lucy!' Charles advised. 'The big chief has wedding plans of his own. Shall you come to the farewell-Mark-welcome-Iris party?'

'I expect so.' Lucy felt heavy-hearted at the very thought. 'And you?'

'Oh, I'll come for an hour maybe. Tamsin wants me to look at a likely house, so I may be late.'

'Where's Dr Morton staying in the meantime?' Lucy asked.

'The guest suite.' Charles winked. 'Dr Roxburgh's always around there, seeing to her comfort.'

'You still don't like him?'

'Dr Roxburgh? Oh, let's say I look forward to marriage doing him good!'

'I believe Dr Morton's going to begin on IVF tomorrow,' said Lucy. 'She's going to assist Dr Roxburgh at the collection.'

'How touching! Will you be there?'

'Of course.'

'Lucky you!' he laughed.

The collection was usually scheduled in Theatre for nine-thirty. The patients had received their gonad-rine injections the previous night, their temperatures and hormone level already checked. Then the delicate extraction operation began.

Lucy watched as the gowned and masked Dr Roxburgh jerked his head for Dr Iris Morton to step nearer. Something about their very posture showed the closeness and trust of their relationship.

Dr Morton came over to watch Lucy as she carefully washed the oocytes for laboratory examination and culture development. Dr Iris's eyes above the mask were bright, intelligent and lively. Even in her distress, Lucy could recognise why Dr Roxburgh loved her.

When they had scrubbed up, Dr Morton followed her out of surgery. 'So you're Lucy!' Dr Morton said reflectively, and put out her hand. 'You didn't stop to be introduced the other day.'

Lucy felt discomfited. 'When you arrived, no. I had. . . I had to see someone. We were late.'

'And I was early,' Dr Iris laughed.

And you went on hugging for so long, Lucy added—but only to herself.

'Are you coming to our party?' asked Iris.

'Yes, I hope so.'

'Good! I'll see you then. I've heard a lot about you.'

'And we've heard a lot about Dr Iris,' laughed Meg, when Lucy told her that evening. 'The buzz is that the wedding-day's been fixed.'

Lucy shrugged. 'Oh?'

'Always remember,' Meg offered cheerfully, 'there are more fish in the sea than ever came out.'

Lucy shook her head.

'The trouble is, you've got hooked on one particular fish!'

Lucy laughed, and changed the subject. 'What are you going to wear for the party?' she asked.

Fenella came in and they sorted through their wardrobes.

But even that evening their thoughts were not really on the party. Meg began pressing her red caftan because Andrew liked it. But all three of them were pondering another rumour that had begun circulating—this time to the effect that the tests done on Little Boy Blue were disturbing.

The following day Rupert Roxburgh confirmed the news. After morning clinic he came into Lucy's office with a sheaf of lab reports in his hand.

'I want to make one last attempt to find Boy Blue's mother,' he told her without preamble. 'Buzz Mrs Parsons, will you, and get her in on this?'

He paced up and down Lucy's office while she rang Mrs Parsons, flicking the lab reports against the back of his hand in exasperation.

'She's just coming,' Lucy told him.

'Good!' He frowned in concentration, his brows just lifting a second to nod as Mrs Parsons opened the door. 'Thanks for coming so promptly.'

He waved her to the chair in front of Lucy's desk, propping himself against the radiator. 'Boy Blue's going to need a lot of treatment, including a possible marrow transplant.'

'So he's not going to be fit for adoption?' Mrs Parsons asked.

'No.'

'Never?'

'In my opinion, never.'

'So it's keeping him here till he's fit to go to a children's home?'

'I'm afraid so,' Rupert said sadly.

'Ironic, isn't it,' said Lucy, 'that loving parents are what he needs right now, and that's what he can't have.'

She heard her voice shake, and Dr Roxburgh seemed to jump on that momentary weakness.

'The last thing he wants is for us to get emotional, Sister!' he snapped. He drew a deep breath. 'The most important thing is to find the baby's mother.'

'How?' Mrs Parsons asked. 'The police have done their level best, but they've no leads at all.'

'We must appeal to her.'

'We have done—in the Press, on the radio, by handbills.'

'No good! We need to get to her visually.'

'Television?' Lucy suggested.

'Exactly! I'm glad you agree. I've already had a word with the local television director, and he'll co-operate. So it's all arranged.'

'Splendid!' Mrs Parsons clapped her hands. 'The sooner the better. When do you go on?'

'Oh, I don't, Mrs Parsons. I'm no actor—I'd be

no good. The person to go on will be Sister here.
She found the baby. She can hold it in her arms in
front of the cameras. I'm sure,' Rupert Roxburgh
finished drily, 'when she wants to she can melt
anyone's heart.'

'Except the right one,' Lucy murmured, but not
loud enough for Dr Roxburgh to hear.

'Very well,' he said briskly, 'that's agreed. The
crew will be here this afternoon.'

That afternoon a small audience gathered in the
corner of the nursery, where Lucy sat with Boy Blue
in her arms, facing the mobile television cameras.

'Just speak from the heart,' the man in charge of
the crew told her. 'Don't try to follow a script.'

'After all,' Dr Roxburgh interrupted, 'there's only
one major point to get across. Tell the mother,
whoever she is, and wherever she is, to come forward. We need to keep the baby in hospital, but we
need her to be with him. No action at all will be
taken against her. There's the special line,
Hartington 7634, which will be kept open for her,
and for her alone.'

After that injunction, Dr Roxburgh retired behind
the cameras and stood with his arms folded over his
chest.

The cameras rolled. He watched Lucy, his eyes
narrowed, his expression unreadable.

It wasn't, after all, difficult to speak from the
heart. Lucy found herself pleading so hard that,

despite Dr Roxburgh's dictum about not getting emotional, the tears ran down her cheeks.

She couldn't remember what she said. She knew she began by explaining that the little boy needed bone marrow, and the mother's, and hers alone, might be suitable. She could vaguely remember saying something about the baby's need for love, everyone's need for love, that everyone feared rejection, so how much harder to bear was it for a small sick child to be rejected by his mother.

At the end, Meg and Mrs Parsons were misty-eyed. Dr Roxburgh looked studiously unemotional.

'You were absolutely marvellous!' Charles told Lucy.

The man on the rostrum wiped his eyes with the back of his hand. 'Just what the doctor ordered! You'll have the audience in floods. Ratings'll go up, I shouldn't wonder.'

'Sorry about the tears,' Lucy apologised.

'Lovey, they'll go down a treat! Real raw emotion! They'll lap it up!'

Dr Roxburgh said nothing. Travelling down on the escalator back to her office, Lucy felt a hand on her arm.

Rupert Roxburgh said, 'Thank you. Let's hope it gets results.' And then in a different tone, as they reached the ground floor and walked down the corridor to her office, 'I wonder if all those tears were for Little Boy Blue?'

'I've no idea what you mean,' she said, with her hand on the office doorknob.

'I wonder if they were for yourself as well?'

She drew in her breath sharply. Her eyes sparkled with outrage. Words failed her.

At last she gasped, 'You're impossible!'

She pushed open the door and shut it firmly behind her.

And in the end, like so many tears, they were wasted.

The special line never rang.

Nor had it rung by the afternoon of the farewell/welcome party. 'Well, we can't let it get us down,' Meg said briskly as she and Lucy shampooed each other's hair and prepared for the evening's celebration.

'At least we can be thankful for the Armitages,' Lucy said with determined cheerfulness.

She had no desire to go to the party, but she had to confess to herself that, as the hateful doctor had suggested, some of the sadness was selfish. To watch him officially welcoming his fiancée would be rubbing salt into an intractable wound.

'I'm glad you're wearing that,' said Meg as Lucy hung up her blue silk dress. 'It suits you. Goes with your eyes.'

'Dr Iris has very vivid blue eyes,' Lucy murmured.

'So?'

'So nothing, really.'

'Well, hurry up! The boys will be round with the taxi in a moment!'

'Are we all going to squeeze in?' queried Lucy.

Fenella came down from her room at that moment, wearing a smart pencil-slim black and white dress with matching black and white earrings and black patent leather shoes. The other two drew in their breaths approvingly.

She flushed with pleasure. 'Bill's making his own way there,' she said.

'Ready to breathalyse everyone, I shouldn't wonder,' Meg teased.

'There's the taxi horn! Come on—those fellows next door are half starved! They don't want to waste a moment's eating time.'

At least the boys next door kept up everyone's spirits as they crammed in the taxi for the short drive to the hospital.

In the small panelled committee-room where the party was being held, Andrew and Mick found them a table strategically placed near the food buffet. Jim, the radiographer, brought over a staff nurse from Intensive Care, then went off to collect a tray of drinks and a plate of dainty food.

The room filled up quickly, but the atmosphere was subdued. The staff were genuinely sorry to say goodbye to Mark Duffey, even though that farewell might only be temporary, and, though the unit tried hard not to get emotionally involved with patients, the fate of Boy Blue hung over them.

Mark was already going round shaking people by the hand and saying goodbye, and pretending not to notice the expensive leather overnight bag with his initials in gold standing on the drinks table, ready for Rupert Roxburgh to present to him.

When Dr Roxburgh came in, Iris Morton had her arm through his. And somehow the atmosphere of the party visibly lightened. She too was wearing blue—a tight-fitting watered silk, very short number—and some of the livelier research students whistled.

Matron and the chairman of governors followed them in, and engaged the two doctors in conversation quite close to what Andrew called the Laburnum Villas table.

Lucy heard Matron ask in a trumpeting whisper, 'When is the wedding, my dear? We're all dying to know.'

Suddenly Lucy couldn't bear to hear any more.

'I've left my handkerchief in the cloakroom,' she murmured, and escaped.

Outside in the corridor, the door to the quadrangle was open to let in the evening air. The blossom that Dr Roxburgh had remarked on had long since gone, but something scented the air with a haunting fragrance.

She stood in the doorway, staring out.

'What are you running away from, Lucy?' a deep voice asked. A hand was thrust under her elbow, and she found herself gently but firmly propelled out into the courtyard.

'Nothing,' she told Rupert Roxburgh. 'Why should I run from anything?'

'Why indeed? But you ran away before.'

'I told you why. I told you I didn't want to hear what you were going to say.'

He grasped her arm and spun her round roughly. 'Well, you're damned well going to hear this time!'

'No!' she protested.

She tried to pull away from him, but he pinioned her arms to her sides.

'I love you, Lucy.' He bent down and kissed her fiercely on her lips. She had to clench her fists to stop herself throwing her arms round his neck and pressing him to her. 'I love you—I'm in love with you! I want you! And I don't give a damn about anyone else!'

Breathless, angry, tempted, she stammered the one word, 'Iris.'

With unspeakable brutality, he snapped, 'Iris doesn't stop me wanting you! Iris is irrelevant!'

At that point Lucy felt like bursting into tears. So this was the man whom for years she had loved and looked up to. Hated a little, perhaps, resented perhaps, but respected. Here were his feet of clay! A man who was about to marry a clever attractive woman, but who also wanted to have a love-affair with her.

Tears turned to a healthy anger.

'I don't care,' she snapped, 'whether you love me or not! That's irrelevant to me. I couldn't love you if you were the last man on earth!'

Then she turned and fled back through the french doors, tried to disguise the angry flags of colour in her cheeks with face powder, then slid into her chair at the Laburnum Villas table.

'Anyone seen anything of Dr Roxburgh?' Mark was asking. 'Speeches are now on the menu.'

The muscles along Rupert Roxburgh's jaw were tight with anger as he stalked back into the room. But he managed a wide smile at the assembled company.

'Sorry about that,' he said, but offered no excuse.

Then he went over to the drinks table. 'Is everyone's glass charged? Good!' From the table top, he lifted a roll of paper which he shook out till it was about ten feet long. 'My speech,' he smiled humorously.

The research students groaned.

'No, I won't make a speech. Just to say how much we all value Mark, and how well we wish him.'

He then presented the overnight bag, and refrained from making a hospital joke about it.

'And now, Iris!' He took her hand. 'What can I say? I want you all to welcome her because she's a very special person. My brother's a very lucky man. As only a very few of you know, because the appointment was confidential, he's coming within the next few months to the university as Dean of Medicine. And as only Iris and I know, that's a tremendous achievement, because he's been crippled with polio for the last twenty years. I'm in a privileged category with them both, I can claim to be their favourite person, because I introduced them. I persuaded Iris to continue her studies in

America. I'm sorry we haven't anything to present you with, Iris.' He kissed her forehead, and smiled. 'That's just for leavers.'

'Oh, but that's not quite right.' Charles made a dramatic appearance. 'I have a present to welcome Dr and Mrs Morton soon-to-be-Roxburgh.' He held up something that glittered in his hand. 'The keys of my flat! With my blessings! I'm leaving. I'm making other arrangements.'

In the general laughter and congratulations, Lucy sat stunned. Indeed, all three girls sat awed.

'Trust the grapevine to get it right except for the most important part!' Meg, the first to find her voice, said indignantly.

'Well, I'm jiggered!' said Andrew.

Meg struck her own head with the heel of her hand several times, as if trying to kick-start her brain into working.

'So does it mean, Lucy, that Dr Roxburgh isn't going to marry anyone, and if he isn't, then. . .?' But Lucy for the second time had mumbled an excuse and left. Andrew made some joke about her needing to find her handkerchief again, for which Meg kicked him sharply under the table.

Fenella volunteered to go and find her, but Meg shook her head.

'She wants to be on her own,' she said firmly.

In fact, Lucy didn't know what she wanted. Her head was spinning, her heart racing. What had Rupert Roxburgh been saying, and what had she just done?

At best, she had thrown away her chance of happiness, as maybe she had thrown it away before. At worst, she had grossly insulted and made an enemy of the man she loved.

She was not quite sure where she should go— anywhere to get away.

At first she walked along to Palmer Ward and chatted to the two patients who had had their hCG injection and were awaiting oocyte collection in the morning. She calmed their fears as best she could, then lingered for a moment with Sister Ireton, the night sister.

'I'll stay here,' she offered, 'while you have a few minutes at the party.'

'Parties aren't in my line,' Sister Ireton told her. 'But thanks all the same.'

'I don't think they're mine either,' Lucy smiled, sipping the tea Sister Ireton poured for her.

Ten minutes later Lucy was on her way to her favourite place—the nursery. The place that made all their work and all the disappointments worthwhile.

She was just travelling up on the escalator when she saw a figure descending on the other staircase.

The figure was vaguely familiar. It was the figure out of a dream or something half remembered. Suddenly dream and memory came together. It was not just in her dream that she'd seen that figure— the girl with the spiky yellow hair and the tears wet on her face. Furtive tears dashed away with the back of her hand.

The girl at the fête.

Only this time she wasn't crying. Her face was deathly pale but frighteningly determined. And in her arms was a baby, tightly swaddled in a shawl, and fiercely held.

They passed at mid-floor, exchanging a horrified glance. Then the escalator inexorably continued sweeping Lucy upwards and the girl downwards.

The mother of Little Boy Blue had responded all right. But not to come and stay with him, but to snatch him away, which might prove his death sentence.

All Lucy knew was that she mustn't cry out. Mustn't sound the alarm. Mustn't this time run or hurry or startle the girl into running out into the night. She had to hurry, but not seem to hurry. She had to be calm. She had to stay, against all her instincts, quiet and not cry out. By the time she had alighted from the upward escalator, the girl had set foot in the hall, was hurrying for the glass doors and the anonymity of the night. Lucy swiftly stepped to the descending escalator.

The security guard in the glass entrance box was talking into the telephone, not even glancing in the direction of the hall.

There was no one to stop the girl.

It was then Lucy saw a seemingly totally relaxed figure just by the door. Dr Roxburgh had his hands in his pockets, and was smiling as if totally unaware that anything was wrong. At first Lucy thought he had simply not taken in what was happening, had assumed the girl was a late visitor.

Then as the downward escalator took Lucy back to the hall, she saw him slowly stretch out his hands, smile and say something.

The girl stopped, hesitated. That was the vital moment when Boy Blue's future hung on a thread. The girl seemed poised for swift and immediate flight, yet Dr Roxburgh made no attempt physically to detain her. For a few seconds they stayed talking quietly, then suddenly the girl put Boy Blue into his arms.

Lucy half expected the girl to then bolt out of the door, but she didn't.

Dr Roxburgh held the baby comfortably in the crook of one arm, and the other he put round the girl. Together, unhurriedly, almost companionably, they walked over to the escalator, as Lucy stood rooted to the spot.

Only then did Dr Roxburgh acknowledge her presence.

'Well, Lucy,' he said, 'aren't you going to come and complete the family? Or are you and I forever going to be sweeping past each other on opposing escalators?'

'That,' said Lucy, hours later, well past midnight, 'was surely the most unromantic proposal any girl ever had!'

They were walking in the hospital garden. Boy Blue's mother had been given a bed in the hospital.

Their hour-long talk with her had been interrupted by the arrival of the Armitages. Matron had phoned them to say the boy's mother had been found. On the way to the hospital, the never-say-die Armitages had thought up a scheme. Here was a role for them. They would adopt mother *and* baby, if the girl were willing.

So far, she was. She looked dazed at this sudden turn of events, but happy. Suddenly hope of a new life seemed to beckon for them both.

Now the moon was full. It shone softly on the little statue of Eros and bathed the scrubby lawn in cosmetic silver. Lucy and Rupert stood under the shadow of the oak tree.

'Who said it was a proposal, Lucy, darling?'

'Your eyes,' she said. 'Your voice. Something about you.'

'Why didn't they tell you before?'

'They did. But I didn't believe them.'

'You believed your little room-mate?'

'Nesta,' Lucy sighed. 'I shouldn't have done.'

'And then you believed the hospital grapevine.'

'So did you. About me and Charles.'

'Oh, there was some evidence too,' Rupert said severely. 'In fact, *considerable* evidence. The Riverside, your house, his flat, even your office! Besides, you told me you loved someone else.'

'How did you know I didn't?' she queried.

'I watched your face when I told them all about my brother and Iris, and I knew then. That's why I came to find you yet again.'

'And found Little Boy Blue and his mother?'

'Yes. But this time I really found *you*.' Rupert put his hand under her chin and tilted up her face.

Lucy looked up at him, her blue eyes wide and a little reproachful. 'You seemed to love Iris so much.'

'I do—unashamedly. But not the way I love you.' He put his arms round her and kissed her slowly and tantalisingly, brushing her lips with his.

'Kiss me properly,' she begged.

'Only if you say you'll marry me. Only if you promise you'll believe me as well as love me.'

'Oh, I will,' she said. 'I will!'

PENNY JORDAN

A
COLLECTION

From the bestselling author of *Power Play*, *Silver* and *The Hidden Years* comes a special collection of three early novels, beautifully presented in one volume.

Featuring:

SHADOW MARRIAGE
MAN-HATER
PASSIONATE PROTECTION

Available from May 1992   Priced £4.99

W☉RLDWIDE

Mills & Boon

Discover the thrill of 4 Exciting Medical Romances – FREE

FREE BOOKS FOR YOU

In the exciting world of modern medicine, the emotions of true love have an added drama. Now you can experience four of these unforgettable romantic tales of passion and heartbreak FREE – and look forward to a regular supply of Mills & Boon Medical Romances delivered direct to your door!

🌾 🌾 🌾

Turn the page for details of 2 extra free gifts, and how to apply.

An Irresistible Offer from Mills & Boon

Here's an offer from Mills & Boon to become a regular reader of Medical Romances. To welcome you, we'd like you to have four books, a cuddly teddy and a special MYSTERY GIFT, all absolutely free and without obligation.

Then, every month you could look forward to receiving 4 more **brand new** Medical Romances for £1.60 each, delivered direct to your door, post and packing free. Plus our newsletter featuring author news, competitions, special offers, and lots more.

This invitation comes with no strings attached. You can cancel or suspend your subscription at any time, and still keep your free books and gifts.

Its so easy. Send no money now. Simply fill in the coupon below and post it at once to -

Mills & Boon Reader Service, FREEPOST, PO Box 236, Croydon, Surrey CR9 9EL

NO STAMP REQUIRED

- - - ✂ -

YES! Please rush me my 4 Free Medical Romances and 2 Free Gifts! Please also reserve me a Reader Service Subscription. If I decide to subscribe, I can look forward to receiving 4 brand new Medical Romances every month for just £6.40, delivered direct to my door. Post and packing is free, and there's a free Mills & Boon Newsletter. If I choose not to subscribe I shall write to you within 10 days - I can keep the books and gifts whatever I decide. I can cancel or suspend my subscription at any time. I am over 18.

EP20D

Name (Mr/Mrs/Ms) _____

Address _____

_____

_____ Postcode _____

Signature _____

mps
MAILING
PREFERENCE
SERVICE